All That's Left to You

All That's Left to You

A Novella and Short Stories

by Ghassan Kanafani
translated by *May Jayyusi and Jeremy Reed*

with an introduction by Roger Allen

Interlink Books

An imprint of Interlink Publishing Group, Inc.
Northampton, Massachusetts

This edition first published in 2023 by

INTERLINK BOOKS
An imprint of Interlink Publishing Group, Inc.
46 Crosby Street, Northampton, Massachusetts 01060
www.interlinkbooks.com

Originally published in Arabic as *Ma tabaqqa la-kum*, Beirut, 1966

ISBN 978-1-62371-724-7

This English translation is published with the cooperation of PROTA (the Project of
Translation from Arabic); director: Salma Khadra Jayyusi, Cambridge, Massachusetts, USA

Printed and bound in the United States of America

9 8 7 6 5 4 3 2

Table of Contents

Acknowledgments

I would like to acknowledge the contribution made by Issam al-Tahir and Omar Bakir towards the translation of the short stories in this book and towards the preparation of a final publisher's copy. Their generosity made it possible for PROTA to offer to the English-speaking reader some of the most sensitive and artistically viable selections of fiction in contemporary Arabic letters, and I thank them very much for this.

The translation of *All That's Left to You* was volunteered by May Jayyusi, and the costs towards the second translation of this novella were graciously contributed by Ali Qasid, himself an admirer of Kanafani. I want to thank both of them warmly for giving us the chance to bring out this famous Kanafani work in English. My thanks go also to Jeremy Reed, poet and novelist, and an ardent translator of good literature. His enthusiastic support for PROTA has been invaluable and has helped enhance my determination to continue with the task of producing the works of our best authors in English translations.

My gratitude also goes to Amin Abd al-Hafiz for helping us out with the checking of the final translations, which he did with precision and zeal; and to Christopher Tingley, friend, stylist and great lover of literature, for his meticulous assistance in helping me, at a time of great need for help, put the final touches on this and many other PROTA works.

My colleague, Roger Allen, who wrote the introduction to this English collection, deserves many thanks. This is not the only labor of love which he has offered to PROTA, and his continued care and support have been indispensable. It is serious scholars like him that make collegiate collaboration conducive not only to the success of the work but also to the health and joy of those who do it.

Salma Khadra Jayyusi
Director, PROTA

Introduction

The period following the Second World War has been one of dramatic change for the nations and regions of the Arab World. For many nations the struggle for independence, revolution, social change, economic development and confrontation with former colonizers and new world powers have all provided vehicles for both discussion and action. In the way in which the challenge of these forces has been faced, each nation and region can present a different history. However, one event during this time period—the War of 1948 as a result of which the State of Israel emerged—created a sense of shock and consequent unity which has maintained the plight of the Palestinian people as the major topic of Arab litterateurs throughout the Arabic-speaking region. While the emergence in the Arab World of the literary rallying cry known as the *iltizam*, "commitment" (a transfer to the region of the ideas of Western authors, prime amongst whom was Sartre) may have been in process before this event, there is little doubt that, as the movement gathered momentum in the 1950s, the Palestinian cause became its primary motivating factor. The passage of four decades has done nothing to alter or diminish the tensions created by the events of 1948; indeed, every new conflict—1956, 1967, 1973 (and as I write, 1989)— has provided further impetus and new avenues of creativity through which writers of literature have broached the topic.

It should come as no surprise to learn that Palestinian writers themselves have been in the forefront of those who have addressed themselves to the tragedy of their own people, and in a variety of genres and styles. Among their number we find authors who write from within Israeli territory itself, some of whom have spent time in prison for their pains. Other writers address themselves to the various aspects of their quest for land and national identity from the Palestinian diaspora, either from one of the other nations of the Arabic-speaking world or from one of the many Western nations to which the more professionally qualified emigrated in search of livelihood. While all these writers display a sense of "commitment" to the cause of their people, there is one author who, in the words of the Egyptian writer, Yusuf Idris, has taken this cause to the utmost limit of martyrdom: Ghassan Kanafani, whose fictional writings are the subject of this anthology.

Born in 1936 in Akka (Acre), Kanafani was part of the 1948 exodus from Palestine. His lawyer father took the family first to Beirut and thence to Damascus, where Ghassan went to school. Initially, he worked as a teacher, most particularly in Kuwait, where he spent the years from 1955 till 1960. The experience of exile from his homeland and the conditions, both personal and societal, of his temporary abode are clearly reflected in the fictional works that he wrote later in his career. In the early 1960s he was persuaded by George Habash, a Palestinian intellectual who was later to become the head of the Popular Front for the Liberation of Palestine (PFLP), to return to Beirut and become a journalist. Beginning with *Al-Muharrir*, a pro-Nasser daily newspaper, he moved to work for *Al-Anwar* after the June War of 1967 and thence to *Al-Hadaf*, the organ of the PFLP itself. At this period he also served as official spokesman for Habash's group. It was while serving in these two capacities and at the same time developing his fictional techniques in a variety of ways that he was killed in 1972. The circumstances involved in his death are clear enough: a time-bomb was placed in his car. What is less clear is who was involved in the atrocity: while most hands pointed to the Israeli secret service, it has to be admitted that relations between the splintered Palestinian and other Arab groups were far from cordial at the time. What is abundantly clear is that, with Kanafani's death, modern Arabic fiction was deprived of a major developing talent. "Those whom the Gods love die young," said Menander long ago, but he surely was not thinking of the unnatural causes of death placed at the disposal of modern man.

* * * * *

Within the realm of modern Arabic fiction, Kanafani's reputation rests to a substantial degree on a single work, *Rijal fi al-shams*, 1956 (translated into English by Hilary Kilpatrick as *Men in the Sun*, 1978). Both theme and novelistic treatment certainly serve to make this novel an important contribution to modern Arabic literature. Its publication date places it within that dark period when Arab states, in many cases relishing an incipient independence and going through periods of often traumatic political and social revolution, had to reconcile themselves to the existence of the State of Israel in their midst and to the fate of the Palestinian people displaced by the events of 1948. In a work of comparative brevity Kanafani manages to capture to the full the combination of anger and despair with which different generations of Palestinians confronted their bleak fate, either within the boundaries of the new Zionist state or in the diaspora of exile from their homeland. The experiences of Abu Qays, Assad and Marwan, as they try to make their way to the Gulf and the prospect of a job, reflect the aspirations and hopes of different generations which are united in their loss of roots in place. The sheer venality which they encounter from the Arabs who people this novel is a poignant commentary by a Palestinian author on the nature of support which they received during this trying period. The one person prepared to help them is Abu Khayzuran, the driver of the water-tank truck, who had been rendered impotent by a wound suffered during the 1948 fighting. At the crucial moment during the border crossing he is delayed by the border guards who, not knowing his "condition," tease him about his girlfriend in Basra while the three Palestinians roast to death inside the truck. "Why didn't they beat on the side of the truck?" Abu Kayzuran wonders as he dumps the bodies on a municipal garbage dump and removes their valuables. The portrayal of suffering and callous indifference is here shown in its most cogent form, and yet the entire work is steeped in a powerful symbolism whereby place—and particulary the earth itself—and time—

represented by the passing of the hours and relentless heat of the daytime sun—become active contributors to the plot of the novel.

Men in the Sun is an undoubtedly powerful work and one which has captured not only the imagination of readers throughout the Arab World but also the attention of the vast majority of critics of the Arabic novel. This attention and acclaim has tended to place *Ma tabaqqa la-kum* (*All That's Left to You*), 1966, the novel translated in this collection, somewhat in the shadow of the earlier work. I should therefore state that, from a critical point of view, I find *Ma tabaqqa la-kum* an equally successful essay in fiction, and indeed, from the point of view of modern experimental techniques in Arabic fiction, a distinct advance. Mention was made above to the role of time and place in *Men in the Sun.* In *All That's Left to You* the author carries the process further by stipulating in a "Clarification" which begins the work that both Time and the Desert are considered as "characters" alongside Hamid, Maryam and Zakaria. He alludes to his experiments with this technique by noting how the treatment of these characters involves a series of disconnected lines which occasionally come together in such a way that they seem to be making just two strands and no more. This process of fusion also involves the elements of time and place, so that there appears to be no clear distinction between places and times which are far removed from each other, or indeed between places and times at a single moment.

Time does indeed play a pivotal role in this novel. The events take place over a period of some eighteen hours, many of them at night, and there is copious use of flashback to provide the reader with details of earlier events in the lives of the principal characters. Time becomes symbolized through the ticking of both the wall clock in the "temporary" Palestinian home on the Gaza Strip where Maryam and her feckless and already married lover, Zakaria, have set up house and also the watch which Maryam's brother, Hamid, carries with him in his journey across the desert to join his mother. The wall clock's beats echo the movements of the unborn child within Maryam's womb which has signalled disaster for this scattered family; and those same pulsations mingle with the footsteps of Hamid as he moves ever further away and closer to their mother. When Hamid discards his watch in the desert, he discovers another pulse, that of the earth itself, a favorite image of Kanafani and, one might add, of the vast majority of Palestinian writers for whom earth now implies alienation from what is most beloved. At several moments in this novel time itself becomes frozen as separate events in two places assume a single symbolic function; and it is here that Kanafani's experiments with narration can be clearly gauged:

> *He had abandoned any kind of reflection and was relying, instead, on senses distorted by terror and excitement. He seemed, from his emotions, like an intrepid adventurer who dares to knock on an unknown gate./* When I saw him at the door, I felt afraid and excited at the same time, and trembled all over. Hamid had left only five minutes before, and Zakaria, self-assured, was standing in the doorway asking, "Is he here?"

The desert and Maryam are both serving as narrators here (we have replicated the different intensities of print to be found in the original through the use of italics here). However, the subtleties of Arabic morphology can convey here something of which English is incapable. For it is immediately obvious to the reader in Arabic that the narrative voice changes with the words "When I saw..." since all the adjectives show the marker of the feminine. The desert is speaking of Hamid in mid-journey, while Maryam recounts the fateful occasion when she succumbed to the temptation which her aged aunt had feared for so long. Brother and sister, separated by age and by distance, are now united in a common struggle, the symbolism of which becomes even more forceful when Hamid ambushes an Israeli border guard. Each faces an "enemy," the one within and the other without. As the novel proceeds, the narrative pace quickens:

> **Once again I found myself facing a situation I couldn't cope with, a predicament which made me first smile, then suddenly burst out into laughter.**/ Zakaria turned over and looked at me. Then he went back to sleep, as though he too felt himself submerged in an insane dream./ **"Perhaps you only know Hebrew, but that doesn't matter. But really, isn't it amazing that we should meet so dramatically here in this emptiness, and then find that we can't communicate?"** He went on looking at me, his face dark and hesitant and somewhat suspicious, but there was no doubt he was afraid. As for me, I'd crossed the barrier of fear, and the emotions I was feeling were strange and inexplicable.

This passage not only illustrates further switching in the narrative voice, but also involves changes in person and time-frame. The effect on the reader is not a little cinematic and not a little disorienting. However, as the narrative progresses, the intrinsic uncertainties of the narrative and the intrusion of Time and Place as "characters" resolve those feelings and leave behind the imprint of a most successful experiment in narrative synchronicity.

In the wake of the appalling defeat of 1967, the so-called *naksa* ("setback"), many things were changed for ever in the Arab World. A period of intense and agonizing soul-searching, settling of accounts with both present and past and plotting of future developments was the result of this wholesale disaster. In the case of Ghassan Kanafani's fiction it led to a more direct focus on specific issues; there is now less concern with the creative experiments of such works as *All That's Left to You* and more interest in a type of narration akin to reportage. Those interested in the development of narrative techniques in modern Arab fiction may have cause to regret this shift in focus in one who was clearly involved in significant experimentation, but it has to be admitted that, with *Im Saad* (1969), we have one of the most memorable portrayals in the realm of Arabic fiction concerning the Palestinian people. In this case we are dealing with a very particular kind of "novel." Kanafani tells his readers that Im Saad is a real person, and we may therefore assume that her young interviewer and interlocutor is a reflection of Kanafani himself. This "factual" base is cleverly woven into a narrative framework of episodes whereby the quintessentially traditional Palestinian mother, given identity through her son Saad, who joins the *fidayin*, gradually becomes aware of the dimensions of the situation in which she and her fellow camp-dwellers are and seem liable to remain without further action. The skillful use of the separate episodes to illustrate this gradual process of increasing awareness is the principal evidence here of Kanafani's fictional gifts, even though they are now applied in a more directly political fashion.

In another novel published one year later, Kanafani was to address himself to a number of issues connected with the situation of himself and other Palestinians in *Aid ila Haifa* (*Returning to Haifa*), 1970. An Arab couple, who in their rush to leave Haifa in the fighting of 1948 abandoned an infant son, Khaldun, return to discover that he has been adopted by a Jewish couple who are survivors from the German concentration camps. Now called Dov and brought up Jewish, he refuses to acknowledge his natural parents and insists that he is by upbringing a citizen of Israel. Quite apart from the description and discussion of the events of 1948, this novel also illustrates clearly many other aspects of the conflict, not the least of which is that the Arab couple's other son, Khalid, is eager to join the *fidayin*. In this case, brothers may end up fighting each other.

The Six-Day War of 1967 was a watershed for modern Arabic culture in general, and it is therefore not surprising to notice the differences in focus and technique between Kanafani's pre- and post-67 fiction. At the time of his murder in 1972 three novels, *Al-Ashiq* (*The Lover*), *Al-Ama wa-al-atrash* (*The Blind and the Deaf*), and *Barquq Nisan* (*April Anemones*), were unfinished. In their different ways, each suggests that, had he lived to continue his writing career, the tradition of the Arabic novel would have been provided with further experiments in narrative technique and other contributions to a more explicitly committed literature.

* * * * *

Several authors of modern Arabic fiction have tried their hand at both the novel and the short story, but I believe it fair to suggest that few have been equally successful at both. Writing fiction has never provided a sufficient income to serve as a full-time occupation for litterateurs in the Arab World and does not do so now. Very few have been able to find the time, opportunity or application to develop the time-consuming craft of novel writing for a sustained period; those who have done so have normally held posts as civil servants (as with Najib Mahfuz) or as journalists or writers for some other medium (as with Kanafani, among many others). As a partial result of this situation, the short story has increased in popularity in recent decades, surpassing poetry in many Arab countries. Popular appeal does not always bring about distinguished works of literature, and such has been the case in the Arab World as elsewhere. However, a number of Arab authors have developed the craft of the short story in different ways and produced collections of very high quality. They have come to recognize the extreme artistry required to produce a finely crafted and constructed piece of short fiction which manages to draw readers into its circumscribed and economical environment, and, through the power of concise and allusive language, to show "a slice of life," paint a scene, portray a character or reflect a mood. Life has no short stories of its own, and so the genre is, in the literal sense, an artificial and self-conscious one. The short story is more concerned, it seems, with state than with the processes of change. When the story is over, few things will have been altered, except, one hopes with a great short story, the reader's own perceptions. One has only to read examples of the artistry of great short-story writers, including Zakariyya Tamir or Yusuf Idris among Arab authors, to see the much discussed craft of short-story writing illustrated in a masterly fashion. Arab novelists such as Najib Mahfuz, Jabra Ibrahim Jabra, and Abd al-Hakim Qasim have all seemed equally at home in either genre, and to that list one can certainly append the name of Ghassan Kanafani.

Kanafani published four collections of short stories: *Mawt Sarir 12* (*Death of Bed 12*), 1961; *Ard al-burtuqal al-hazin* (*Land of Sad Oranges*), 1963; *Alam laysa la-na* (*A World Not for Us*), 1965; and *An al-rijal wa-al-banadiq* (*About Men and Rifles*), 1968. The title of the final collection may be seen as part of a wider process of reaction to the Six-Day War, but also reflects the general shift in direction which we noted above in reference to the novels. However, the fate of Palestine and its people is certainly not the only or even the predominant theme of Kanafani's short stories. Indeed, one of the primary features of these collections and of the current excellent anthology culled from them is their variety, most particularly in venue and characters. With regard to place, it seems reasonable to suggest that the different settings may be seen as a reflection of Kanafani's own life experiences: from childhood in Beirut and Damascus, via the Gulf to Palestine and the refugee camps. It is to Kuwait that the three Palestinians make their fateful journey in search of livelihood in *Men in the Sun*. It is to the same Kuwait and for the same purpose that the Umani hospital patient, Muhammad Ali Akbar, the subject of the narrator's postulations in "Death of Bed 12" has come.

In "Lulu fi al-tariq" ("Pearls in the Street") a man who has not been able to make a living in Kuwait squanders the money he has been storing up for the journey "home" on some oysters in the desperate hope that one will contain a pearl. We never discover what the very last one contains; the man has a heart attack and dies, and the oyster vanishes.

Among the varied topics and scenarios for Kanafani's fiction one looks in vain for characters drawn from the bureaucratic and educated classes who tend to form the predominant topic of much modern Arabic fiction, as writers place their world within the milieu that they themselves know best. Expressions of cultural alienation and disorientation such as one finds in the works of a Palestinian author like Jabra Ibrahim Jabra are scarcely to be found in Kanafani's fictional writings. His own experiences, coupled with his strongly held political beliefs, led him to concentrate his attentions on the poorer classes, and most particularly on those who live closest to that entity which the Palestinians hold dear, whatever their class: the land. Thus, for Kanafani as for the Palestinian poets, the land is lovingly portrayed, its pulsating rhythms providing a life-giving force to the characters in his fiction. The qualities of these peasants are described with admiration; and on occasion this cast of characters is extended to include the Bedouin, that repository of all traditional lore and values of the Arab nation.

In analyzing Kanafani's short stories, one of the most interesting features to be observed is his concern with structure. For example, "Death of Bed 12" presents the process of compiling a story and then, by telling "the truth," revealing the entire first version as pure fantasy. Other stories begin with a kind of "frame story" which then dovetails, somewhat in the manner of its forebears in the popular literature of earlier periods, into another tale told by one of the characters. While these examples can provide the more obvious examples of Kanafani's interest in the means of satisfying the short story's generic purpose, all the stories in this collection can in different ways show the great variety of which the genre is capable and also Kanafani's ability at making use of its potential.

* * * * *

This collection of Kanafani's fiction provides further evidence to the English-reading public of his status within the history of modern Arabic literature, both as a reflector of the miseries and aspirations of his people, the Palestinians, in whose cause he died, and as an innovator within the broader world of Arabic fiction as a whole. It is to be hoped that this collection will help in the process of bringing his name and his worlds to the attention of a wider readership.

Roger Allen

A Clarification

As will be obvious from the outset, the five characters in this novel, Hamid, Maryam, Zakaria, Time and the Desert, do not move along parallel or conflicting lines. In this work we find instead a series of disconnected lines which occasionally come together in such a way that they seem to be making just two strands and no more. This process of fusion also involves the elements of time and place, so that there appears to be no clear distinction between places and times which are far removed from each other, or indeed between places and times at a single moment.

The difficulty implicit in making one's way through a world which is jumbled in this fashion is one that is freely acknowledged. However, it is clearly unavoidable if the novel is to tell its story, as I fully intended that it should, in a single burst. For that reason I have adopted a sugestion that the points of disjuncture, blending and transition—which usually occur without preliminaries—should be clearly designated. That has been done by changing the typeface at the appropriate point.

It has to be admitted that these changes in typeface impede a key component of the transition process, which is supposed to take place unconsciously and without any indication; it gives the impression of assigning a deliberate order to a world which actually has none. However, previous experiments with this approach have made it clear that compromises of this kind are inevitable.

Ghassan Kanafani

(translated by Roger Allen from the Arabic edition of *Ma tabaqqa lakum*)

All That's Left To You

He could now stare directly at the sun's molten disc, and watch its crimson fireball hang on the rim of the horizon before disappearing into the sea. In a flash it was gone, and the last glowing rays that lit up the path of its descent were extinguished like embers against a grey wall that rose shimmering at first, then turned into a uniform coat of white paint.

Suddenly the desert was there.

For the first time in his life he saw it as a living creature, stretching away as far as the eye could see, mysterious, terrible and familiar all at the same time. The light, retreating slowly as the black night sky descended, played over it and transformed it.

It was vast and inaccessible, and yet the feelings it aroused in him were stronger than love or hate. The desert wasn't entirely mute; it felt to him like an enormous body, audibly breathing. As he set off into it, he felt suddenly dizzy. The sky closed in on him noiselessly, and the city he had left behind dwindled to a black speck on the horizon.

In front of him, as far as the eye could see, the body of the desert was breathing, alive. He felt his own body rise and fall at its breast. In the depths of the black sky-wall that stood up erect before him, panels began to open one after another, revealing the hard, brilliant glitter of stars.

Only then did he realize he wouldn't return. Far behind him, Gaza with its ordinary night disappeared. His school was the first to vanish, then his house. The silvery beach was swallowed up in darkness. For a brief moment the street lights, dim and faint, remained as suspended pinpricks; then they too were extinguished one by one. He continued on his way, hearing the stifled swish of his feet as they met the sand, and, as he did so, he recalled the feelings that always filled his breast whenever he threw himself into the waves: strong, immense, utterly solid, and yet at the same time possessed of a total and shattering impotence.

As he plunged into the night, it was as though he was anchored to his home in Gaza by a ball of thread. For sixteen years they'd enveloped him with these constricting strands, and now he was unraveling the ball, letting himself roll into the night. "Repeat after me: I give you my sister Maryam in marriage — I give you my sister Maryam in marriage—for a dowry worth—for a dowry worth—ten guineas...ten guineas...all deferred...all deferred." Eyes had bored into his back as he had sat in front of the *Shaikh*. Everyone there knew very well that it wasn't that he was giving her away, but that she was pregnant, and that the swine who was to be his brother-in-law was sitting next to him, audibly laughing inside.

All deferred, of course, with the child already pressing against the walls of her womb! Outside the room he took her by the arms. "I've decided to leave Gaza," he said. She smiled, and her mouth with its badly applied lipstick looked like a bloody wound that had suddenly opened up beneath her nose. "Where will you go?" she asked, her mouth still open, as though she wanted to tell him that he couldn't do that. "I'll go to Jordan over the desert." "So you're running away from me?" she said. He shook his head. "You were everything to me, but now you're dishonored, defiled, and I'm deceived...If only your mother was here."

Tomorrow he knew she'd say to the bastard she'd borne, "If only your grandmother was here." And he'd grow up in turn, get married, have children and say to his son, "If only your great-grandmother was here." If only...if only...for sixteen years he'd been saying that to her: "If only your mother was here!" Something he would repeat whenever they quarreled, when they laughed, when she was in pain, when she didn't know how to cook, when they fired him from his job, when he got work, always the same phrase would occur: "If only your mother was here, if only your mother was here."

His mother had never been there, even though she was only a few hours walk away in Jordan, a distance no one in sixteen years had succeeded in crossing. Even while he was saying, "I give you my sister Maryam in marriage," he had resolved, unconsciously, to make the journey.

He was on fire, tasting a deep bitterness right down to the pit of his stomach, while she stepped back a little, still wearing that wounded smile. Behind her, the swine growled, so she said to him, "Your brother-in-law Hamid wants to leave Gaza." But the other man never so much as looked at him, treating him as though he wasn't there. "Hamid says a lot of things, there's no need to take him seriously." At the same instant he asked himself, 'I wonder where it happened?' He looked at the gentle curve of her belly beneath the dress.

One day, no doubt, he left school early, probably he got permission from the headmaster, saying he had a headache. That was always his way: to plead a headache, and then sneak to the house in my absence, and she'd be waiting for him. There he undid the buttons of her blouse and she pretended to feel nothing. But when?

She turned round without a word, and began talking absently to the guests: "May you enjoy the same." A word rang out—congratulations...congratulations. Cold hands reached out to shake his own, while his eyes were focused on her. Fired by his boiling rage, for two months he'd taken refuge in the fantasy of killing her. He'd imagine himself rushing to her bed, armed with a long knife, uncovering her face; then while she looked up at him with eyes like a madwoman's, he'd grab her by the hair, and say something brief yet cuttingly final—or else he wouldn't speak at all, but just look at her so that she understood everything, and stab her straight through the heart. Then he'd rush outside to look for him, his brother-in-law. "I give you my sister Maryam in marriage for a dowry worth ten guineas, all deferred." His brother-in-law...

She'd allowed this man to tarnish her; her fifteen minutes of surrender had denied the bond between them. When the intruder had planted the child in her womb, he'd had him where he wanted him. "You're free to marry her off to me or not. I'm not the one who'll suffer." "But why didn't you say you wanted her?" He had just shaken his head, smiling like an honest merchant. "It just happened this way." He'd felt like standing up and hitting him, but the man had gone on smiling. "You don't want to hit me, do you? They'll say that you hit the man who..."

Enough!

The man was slight and ugly as a monkey, and he was called Zakaria. Hamid could, if he'd wanted, have put his big hands round him and squeezed him to death, but he was powerless to act; his sister Maryam was listening behind the door, with the child growing all the while in her womb. When the last guests had left, his brother-in-law shut the door and came back in as though he owned the house. He flung off his shoes, and stretched out in a chair, looking like an accidental blemish that didn't belong there. He took a deep breath, clasped his hands behind his head, and stared with malign contentment at the objects in the room. At last his eyes came to rest on her, and he began speaking, exaggerating the contours of his mouth. "So he wants to go, he intends to cross the desert...He hasn't congratulated me yet, even though I'm his brother-in-law—to say nothing of the fact that I'm older than him." Then he jumped up and began pacing around the room, eyes trained on the floor. "He's threatening us, Maryam, so why don't you tell him we don't care about him?" But she'd stood silently leaning against the wall, looking for all the world like an old woman who's just remarried. He stopped and looked at her again, striking the pose of an eloquent orator. "In one night the desert swallows up ten like him." He turned his back on him and faced her: "First he has to cross our borders, then theirs, and theirs again, before he finally arrives at the frontier with Jordan, and these are just small dangers compared

4

with the endless deadly threats the desert holds in store...are you sure this isn't one of his stupid jokes?" She didn't answer and the atmosphere in the room grew tense and oppressive.

A thread of sweat darkened Hamid's collar. He realized he was breathing heavily. If he spoke out he would, he knew, appear ridiculous, but he couldn't help himself. He got up from his chair, headed straight for the door, and then at the right moment swung round, "I'll leave tomorrow night."

As he went down the steps, he wanted to hear a sound, to hear his sister's voice calling out to him—"Hamid, come back." He wanted her to cry out, to say something. But the only sound he heard was the sound of his own footsteps clattering down the stairs. Even before he'd reached the street, he heard the door slam behind him. No solicitous word broke the silence.

The darkness was uniform now. A cold wind had sprung up and was whistling across the surface of the desert, its rhythm like the gasps of a dying beast. He no longer knew whether he was afraid or not. There was one heart beating in the reaches of the sky, in that universal body stretching to the rim of the horizon. He stood still for a while, staring at the perforated black tent of the sky, while the expanse of the desert stretched out dark as an abyss. He pulled up his coat collar and thrust his hands deep into his huge pockets. Suddenly, his fear melted away. He was alone with the creature that was with him, under him and within him, breathing in an audible whistle, as it floated sublimely out on a sea of studded darkness. When a roar reached him from the distance, he greeted it without surprise. Nothing in this vast expanse had the power to shock him; it was a world open to everything, and whatever sound came to him could only be small, clear and familiar. At first the noise had seemed to come from all four quarters, then he was able to distinguish its source. A straight beam of light swept the rim of the horizon like a white stick describing a semicircle. In the next instant two shining eyes were narrowing in on him, bouncing as they came forward with a circular motion. Without fear and without hesitation, he flung himself to the ground and felt it like a virgin quiver beneath him. The strip of light brushed the sand dunes softly, silently. Instinctively, he flattened himself into the sand and felt its soft warmth rise to meet him. The roar was on him now as the car accelerated forward. He dug his fingers into the flesh of the earth, feeling its heat flowing into his body. It seemed to him that the earth was breathing directly into his face, its excited breath burning his cheek. He pressed his mouth and nose against it and the mysterious pounding mounted, while the car suddenly turned and sped by, its rear lights receding redly into the night. "I give you my sister Maryam in marriage." He laid his cheek on the sand again and felt a cold breeze wash over him. The red taillights had disappeared, as though a hand had wiped them out. If only my mother was here, he reflected. He turned and brushed his lips against the warm sand. "It's not in my power to hate you, but how can I love you? In one night you'd swallow up ten like me. I choose your love. I'm forced to choose your love. You're all that's left to me."

You're all that's left to me, and even though you share my bed, you're irretrievably distant. You leave me alone to count the cold metallic strokes beating against the wall. Beating, beating insistently, inside that wooden bier opposite the bed. He'd bought it one July. He'd carried it back from the market, and when he'd got to the door, he couldn't get the keys out of his pocket. It was heavy in his arms, as he told me, and he stood there, perplexed, wondering what to do. Then he forgot himself and remained standing there till I arrived. When he looked at me, sweat was pouring off his body, but he showed no anger. He just said to me, "Why are you late?"

"I'm not late...what's that?"

He looked at it. "It's a wall clock, but it's like a small bier, isn't it?" When we entered, he went straight to the room where we slept. There was a big nail fixed directly opposite his bed and he hung the clock on it, while I held the chair for him. He got down, stood back and admired it. But it didn't work. As he contemplated the clock face, I said to him, "Perhaps it needs winding." He shook his head in disagreement. "I think it's because it's not hanging straight," he said. "Wall clocks with pendulums go wrong if they're tilted." He climbed on the chair again and altered its angle, as though he were preparing to take precise aim at a target. The next instant it began ringing. We both noticed that its metallic strokes were like the sound made by the tapping of a solitary cane. When we put the chair back in its old place, I came out with the question he must have been anticipating. "How much did you pay for it?" His answer was unexpected. "I didn't buy it," he said. "I stole it." And ever since it's been hanging there with its cold metronomic beat. It goes on remorselessly, Zakaria, measuring time without any letup. And now all that's left to me is you and it. We let him desert us without so much as a word. When I heard his hesitant footsteps on the stairs, I thought he'd return, and I felt torn between him, who stands for the past now, and you who are all my hope for the future. And yet neither of us acted, and he didn't come back. Then you stepped forward and slammed the door, putting an end to everything, and went into the next room. When I followed you, you assured me that he'd come back; that he was too young to take on the desert alone. You said that in time he'd come to see how trivial all this is, however important he thinks it now.

If my mother had been here, he would have taken refuge with her, as I would have done too. There would have been a chance to discuss the problem with her. We wouldn't have erased him from our lives the moment the door closed behind him.

I received his first message from the baker's boy: "I'll be leaving today at sunset. I'll write to you from Jordan, if I ever get there." Appended to this was the small signature "Hamid." The note was as composed as the notes he always wrote if he had to leave the house for some reason—when he'd write "Back soon— Hamid" on the back of his cigarette packet and leave it propped up on the radio where he knew I'd go straightway. But we've deceived him, Zakaria. We've deceived him, let's admit it! He'll have been walking for a good three hours by now. I'm counting his steps, one by one, with the subdued metallic strokes on the wall in front of me. It's like a death march.

They are strokes charged with life which he beats out end-lessly against my breast. But my breast gives no echo back, it holds nothing but terror. As he struggles on against the black wall that towers above him, he seems a paltry creature, resolved on an endless journey charged with fury, sorrow, suffocation, even perhaps death, night's solitary song that parades my body. From the moment I felt his approach, I knew he was a stranger; and when I saw him, my suspicions were confirmed. He was totally alone, unarmed, and perhaps hopeless too. Despite that, in that first moment of terror, he said that he asked for my love because he was unable to hate me.

You won't find it in you to despise me, Zakaria, I know that. You're all that's left to me. As for him, he's gone, all traces of him wiped out, except for the incessant monotony of metallic strokes beating on the wall like a cane that's lost its direction. Counting those strokes is all I've left to do, while you're lost in sleep, within my reach, but as distant as death.

You don't really know him, even though you worked with him for a short while in the tent called the camp school. And neither did he know you. Only I know you both. His opinion of you was always the same, expressed concisely; no experience ever altered it. When we first met you together by chance in the street, I learned that your name was Zakaria, and that you were his colleague at the camp school. When I asked if you were a friend, he said; "No, he's a swine." Even when he found out, he just said, "He's a swine!" and left. That was all. He never ever changed this term. "He's a swine."

For the brief intermission of a second, the clock missed a beat before chiming nine, which meant that he must have been walking for three hours in the desert. He never knew that three days later you stopped me in the street and said, "Give my greetings to Hamid," a message I kept to myself because I knew it was just a pretext for your interest in me.

He came to an abrupt halt, looking first at the sky and then at his watch. Like all those who try to escape, he was, I knew, resolved to cover as much ground as possible before the light of dawn arrived. I was spread out beneath him; without hesitation I submitted to his youth as his steps beat into my flesh. But he was just like all the rest, afraid of the infinite expanse, of a horizon without hill, landmark or path. He stood there looking at the uniform blackness of the sand and sky, staring at a spot which lay directly at his feet. Then just as suddenly, he went on, youth that he was, bitter with the contradictions that raged inside him. I couldn't tell him that, by deviating just that little bit towards the south, he had embarked on a course that would lead him by the morning to the heart of the desert and the sun.

I never knew why my feet led me that evening towards the café you used to go to, nor why I slowed down so that you could see me and follow me. How could I know that that momentary prompting would lead me, four months later, to your bed opposite that hanging bier which still beats on. To his bed. This is his bed. We both slept in this room, when our aunt had her own quarters, till she died. My bed was laid out beneath the window. His was on the other side opposite the clock. When our aunt died, I moved my bed to the outer room, and he remained here in his usual place, listening to the constant metallic beat of the clock, as the pendulum moved to and fro, across the wall, without a moment's respite.

When my aunt died, it was on his bed. It seems to me as I look back now that he deliberately worked things like that, because when she was in the throes of her final illness, he suddenly decided to transfer her from the other room to his bed, without explaining why. She died there at one o'clock in the morning by the clock's solitary chime. She must have sensed it, for that single abrupt stroke was the final sound that led her into the thrall of death. She looked at the clock, then looked at me while she went on talking to him. "Greet my sister," she said. "One day, God willing, you'll go to her or else she'll come to you." Ignoring the chime, she gazed at the clock as it started ticking again, and said, "Take care of the girl." It was then that I left the room. The girl, the girl, the girl...she was always in my clothes, in my burning body, in my bed. That girl was stranger than death...

I wasn't aware she'd left the room, but my aunt knew. With one frail finger she pointed at the door through which she'd gone. "Marry her off, Hamid," she said. "Marry her off. She's a girl and I know."

But the slut couldn't wait. She came to me with a child throbbing in her womb. And the father? That dog Zakaria, who'd connived at deceiving me and then forcing me out, while I was drowning in her shame. "I give you my sister Maryam in marriage, I give you my sister Maryam in marriage...all deferred...deferred." She came up to me, "I want to confess something terrible to you," she said. My heart raced as I told her to sit down. When she sat down and folded her hands across her lap, I knew instantly. Terror welled up in me and big drops of sweat stung my eyes. I imagined cries were coming from beneath her hands and from the wound between her thighs which she seemed to be concealing by the position of her hands. When she began to cry softly, I said: "O God, I know." She placed my hands between hers and rubbed them against her lips and tear-runneled face, and swore: "But we will marry, Hamid, we will marry!" Half out of my mind, I kept asking, "Who is he?" "Zakaria!" "Zakaria? Who? Zakaria? O God!"

There was a high wall behind the camp, and they led us all to it. While we thronged the narrow passage that led to the gutted building, they lashed out at us in Hebrew and broken Arabic, alternately. Then they stood us in a line and scrutinized us carefully, at the same time placing the muzzles of their rifles beneath their armpits and standing at ease. Without warning, a slow drizzle began to fall. Behind us the camp was plunged into a black silence. At noon an officer came forward and called out "Salim"; but the line maintained its wet, silent, unbending discipline. When he called out again in his high-pitched voice, someone shuffled his legs, making the pebbles momentarily rattle, before the silence fell again. His patience at an end, the officer seemed a mass of impotent fury. Behind him, deployed like musicians who accompany a well-performed play, the guards released the safety catches on their rifles in unison. The officer slowly drew back, leaving the way for their uninterrupted aim. "If you're so determined to hide the guilty party, then you can all go to hell. We know he's standing there with you!" Once again there was a grating of pebbles as I closed my eyes in an effort to make the world disappear. As I did this, Zakaria rushed out of the straight line and threw himself on his knees, hands drawn to his breast, and began shouting. Slowly, hesitantly, the guns were lowered as the officer strode forward and kicked Zakaria—leaving it to me, with the help of two soldiers, to raise him to his trembling feet again. "I'll show you Salim," he volunteered. But before he could do that, Salim stepped forward of his own accord and stood directly in front of us. He confronted us with an unforgettable look of gratitude as they marched him off, turning around only to fix Zakaria with the countenance of a man who was already dead and about to announce the birth of a ghost. We heard the single shot fired behind the wall and, simultaneously, we all turned our eyes on Zakaria.

Zakaria, Zakaria! My body was on fire beneath my clothes. Even when I took them off and hung them on the wall, the flames continued to feed on those garments. Every morning, as I changed, the clock would sound its melancholy chime from the small bier opposite me. It was then that my wayward breasts would erupt and my hands, unaware, would slide down to my thighs. There wasn't a single large mirror in the house in which I could look at all my body at once. All I could see was my face. When I moved the mirror, the images of my breasts, my belly, my thighs, would appear as a series of disconnected parts belonging to the disembodied figure of a girl being paid the last rites by the merciless mocking beat of the clock's pendulum against the wall. You were the first person to touch me. In that instant, you seemed so close it was as if we had lived in the same clothes together for a lifetime. Beneath the terrible rapping of the aimless cane, submissive to your fingers, your hands, your lips, your eyes, I stripped away thirty-five years of my life piece by piece and year by year. Will I always meet you like a thief, steal glances at you from behind the corners? "Let's get married." "Your brother Hamid will demand a dowry of twenty camel loads." "Ask him." "The boy can hardly stand the sound of my voice. I know him, he'd rather kill you than see you with a man, particularly if it was Zakaria." "Then you don't want to marry me?" "I do, but why don't you want me to see you?"

I've given him everything my untamed nature can afford, and without knowing it, he's gone astray. But there's one thing I can't give him: time. It was sifting through his feet, and not only that, it was working against him. Yet, it wasn't time that he really raced against, but his own loss. Though unconscious of it, he sensed, from his knowledge of my nature, that he must come to a halt. So he stopped. The horizon in front of him was on fire. There were lights, a road and voices in the distance. Had he known he would have realized that he had outdistanced time, but it didn't occur to him. He stood there thinking. His constant movement had warmed his body against the cold wind that cut at him from all directions. Suddenly he spat. I was unconcerned; the depth of his feelings was no business of mine. My concern is with direction, and he'd taken the wrong one, to his great disadvantage. Yet he still seemed to be enraged by something that had no connection with me, or with his standing there half an hour's distance from the right road. Finally, what I had been expecting happened: he avoided the direction of the lights, and once again took a false path, heading in a straight line towards the South. He had abandoned any kind of reflection and was relying, instead, on senses distorted by terror and excitement. He seemed, from his emotions, like an intrepid adventurer who dares to knock on an unknown gate.

When I saw him at the door, I felt afraid and excited at the same time, and trembled all over. Hamid had left only five minutes before, and Zakaria, self-assured, was standing in the doorway asking, "Is he here?" Without waiting for a reply he put a foot inside the door. He entered, placing a hand on my shoulder. I felt its heaviness detaining me. "I want to speak to him about our marriage." A feeling of ecstasy surged through me, and I somehow managed to say: "He isn't here." "Will he be long, I mean, can I wait for him?" he asked. "I don't know," I replied. "I don't think so. It's the first of the month, and he's gone to collect the rations." He walked in then and swung round. "Are you afraid of me?" "No, why should I be?" You came forward and pressed your hard burning lips to my neck, and together we fell on the couch that was my bed. I heard your voice whispering through my clothes, "He'll be late." I felt your hand squeezing my breasts, as your voice went on: "I know he'll be late, I just happened to pass by there." Then your body moved on to me and I was on fire. "I went by the center and there was an unbelievable crowd; it's true, it's the first of the month!" I don't know how I came to feel your rough hands on my bare back. "He'll be late." But the words hardly registered, they hung there meaninglessly; it no longer mattered to me whether he'd be late or not. Then you got dressed and said, "I'd better go." I could feel my body quietly collapsing inside. It was only when the door slammed that I heard the clock striking eight times, as though someone was knocking on the door again. "If only my mother was here, Zakaria, if only my mother was here. But there's no one, only you, and Hamid would kill me if he knew—and I think I'm pregnant." You smiled and put your hand on my shoulder. You looked at my belly as though you could see the child twisting in my entrails, hidden illicitly, viewing the world with two small eyes. Later on, as we delved deep into the maze, you said, "Your body's a fertile land, you little devil, a fertile land, I tell you!"

A fertile land, sown with illusion and unknown prospects. There isn't a steel blade in the world which wouldn't be shattered if it were to graze your naked yellow breast, that bare rugged breast that stretches to eternity, mine and theirs, floating regally in a sea of darkness. All the steel blades of the world could never hack down one root off your surface, but would shatter, one after the other, in the face of your firm harvest which grows bigger and bigger as a man strides further and further into your depth, step-by-step, until he himself turns into a nameless, deep-rooted stem that thrives erect on your juices.

It can't be destroyed. Don't tell me that, even if you think it. I'm so afraid of it I dare not destroy it. It's my shame! Yes it is, Zakaria, my *only* shame in thirty-five virginal, repressed years!

It struck ten. Beating. Beating, as though the cane was forcing itself to move, tapping out its eternal, solitary steps in a small, firmly closed bier. He must have been walking for four hours now, without a moment's pause, and you leave me with him, following his footsteps on the wall, while you lie by my side, deep in sleep. How much further does he have to go? Tell me, Zakaria, Zakaria...

"Aren't you asleep yet?"

"No, tell me, Zakaria, how long does it take a man to cross between Gaza and Jordan on foot?"

"I've told you ten times!"

"No, you haven't."

"Twelve hours!" He turned over for an instant, supporting himself on his side, propped up on one elbow. He listened to the clock strike, then went on. "That's if he knew the way well."

He leaned over, his eyes searching the darkness for my face, and said: "And if he didn't meet up with a patrol in the first hour, then he's all right..."

He was sitting upright now, pushing his hair back with his fingers, and his eyes sprang from his watch to my face. "What's the time now?"

"It's just struck ten."

"I suppose you're thinking of him."

"Yes."

"I tried my best to stop him, in my own way. I hope you're not angry with me?"

"No."

"Then try and go to sleep."

"I've been trying for the past two hours."

He slid deeper into the bed and buried his face in the pillow.

"In any case, it won't help him if you spend the night worrying about what might be happening to him. It's better to stop worrying and go to sleep."

"I'm afraid I can't."

He turned over on his other side and said nothing. Once more the room seemed hollow, punctuated only by the monotony of the clock, which appeared, in its insistence, to be beating against the walls of my skull. Without warning he suddenly leaned over and stretched out his hand for the cigarettes and matchbox on the table. The brief flare lit up his square, rough face, the glint of his small half-closed eyes as they came alive in their dark pits. Leaning on the pillow, he lifted up his body and drew on the cigarette, making a small glow that winked in the darkness before it was eclipsed by the shadow of the tapping cane.

"We'll change as much of the furniture in the house as we can afford to. The beds are good enough, but we'll try and get better chairs for the next room."

"But we have to think of the child first."

"You're obsessed. You'll destroy your youth for him, and in time to come you'll curse the child, and its father, and the time you failed to take good advice. You'll turn into a flabby woman with a stretched belly that looks as though smallpox has been at it. I know these things, I've seen them with my own eyes. For a whole year you won't be a woman, you'll just be a walking milk bottle."

He came closer, putting his cigarette between his lips. He briefly ran his hands over my breast and belly, lingering there, caressingly.

"You've got an amazing body, but you take its beauty for

15

granted. When it's time to give birth, you'll turn into a little mountain of flesh. You'll sacrifice everything for that howling infant who'll make your life hell."

Suddenly she was there. I'd told myself I wouldn't think of her, but now, as he spoke, she came, carrying her children. She stood there at the foot of the bed, as his warm heavy hand was lightly caressing my stomach. I hadn't even asked him her name!

"You never told me her name."

He removed his hand abruptly, and drew heavily on the cigarette. In the magnified silence the solitary step of the clock sounded with increasing urgency.

"I knew you'd ask that one day. I don't mind, of course, but does it have to be now? What made you think of her?"

"Your hand caressing my body. Do you do that to her too?"

"I don't know. Let me give you a piece of advice. For your own peace of mind, try not to think of her."

"What did she say to you?"

"She didn't say anything. She cried too much to be able to talk."

He pulled himself closer to me, and the heat of his breath set me on fire. I knew it was going to happen and I couldn't resist him. My gown slid off beneath his fingers and my nakedness was fluid beneath him. The darkness throbbed with excited hisses. All at once the smell "man" spread out as I began relentlessly undulating, up and down, rhythmically, crushed beneath his shoulders, flung, pushed, pulled, crumpled, left quiet and then dragged, squeezed, kneaded and soaked in water in a terrifying mélange of heat and cold—until, floating over a vortex of unconsciousness, it was Hamid who began shaking me with both hands, gripping my shoulders in his small tense hands, and asking: "Maryam, are you ill?" "No, but where's our mother?" "She was left on the beach. She'll follow later, but our aunt's here with us." He was a little boy and unbelievably courageous. With his sharp eyes he stood gazing at the men, as an equal, not a child, sticking to me as though he were a protective armor against the point of a spear. Beyond the dark beach Jaffa was burning beneath the blazing tails of meteors that thundered down from the sky. We were floating over dark waves of shrieks and prayers. "Why did you leave our mother on the beach?" "I didn't leave her, it was the boat that filled up with people. She'll come in another boat. The men are looking after her. Our aunt and I had to come with you." He was only ten years old, and I was twenty, but even so he seemed to have discovered everything in one mad moment. The whole night he stared at me with the eyes of a young eagle, as we floated in an endless black void, the oars flicking the tops of the waves. Beating. Beating. Jaffa, aglow with flame, slowly receded from view into the infinite expanse of the horizon.

I loved you as I loved myself, you worthless cow. I spent my days engaged in small services to you. I had hoped that one day, as a virtuous woman, you'd marry an honest man. But you opened your thighs to the first worthless man who came along. You let him make you pregnant without considering me for an instant, or his own situation for that matter. You were nothing but a slut. Both of you will rot in his pants. He'll share you both for his pleasure, and there you'll die. I'll tell your mother you died, and I buried you, inside the pants of a rotten man, together with the woman who's borne his five children, and has a sixth on the way.

"So how are we going to live together? Will you stay here with me and leave her? I never asked you that. The whole night may go by without your coming to me, you'll be in her bed. On your way from her house to your school you might knock on my door, or you might not. And each time you go to her you'll pass by my door. O my God! I never realized this house is halfway between hers and your school. Imagine it, seeing you walking in her direction without so much as glancing back at my window. Do you always pull her by the hair as you move up together towards this painful orgasmic climax?"
"I told you to stop thinking about her. Think about me here

with you." He lifted me up in his broad arms, so that I was facing the clock with its invisible hands measuring out time in the dark. We plunged together in rhythmic ecstasy. How can Hamid possibly understand? For all his wonderful manhood, he was my brother. He hadn't yet come to see how important the passing of time was; but to me it was death announcing itself at least twice daily. I was gradually turning day by day into his substitute mother, while day by day he was becoming for me a man who was just a brother. He'd never realized that for me a moment's encounter with a real man would lead to the dissolving of our bond, and the small, beautifully shallow world we'd forced ourselves to choose, a trivial world unprepared to accommodate another spinster. So what did you expect then? Suddenly he tore himself loose, and lay back, naked, panting, while he stared at the ceiling. "You weren't here. I know! You were like a piece of wood. But it won't go on for long. I know how to tame you." He lapsed into silence, letting out an audible whistle. "Fathiyya was like you to start with." "So that's her name—Fathiyya?" "It's typical of you to grasp at nothing but her name. What do you want me to do? Divorce her? Surely you don't need that. You're younger than her and far more beautiful, so why should you be afraid of her? Be patient, and we'll find out what she thinks."

I got up, and the bed creaked. I went to the other room. I once had a young school mate at the English high school, in Jaffa, whose eyes twinkled as she talked, as though she were confiding the secrets of her love life. Her lips seemed voluptuously red and heavy, as if they were regularly kissed. During class, she bit her lips to preserve their glowing color. She was petite, and sheathed in a navy dress; her highly strung body like that of an aroused cat. She was forever writing letters and receiving them, and talking of a man she called "he," and winking conspiratorially. I wonder if time has been kind to you, Fathiyya? Her father always used to say he wouldn't leave Jaffa, even if it turned into a series of stone caves. When he talked, he'd say "welcome" all the time as though he were the hospitable host of a bedouin open house. Once, when we visited her during the troubles, he came into the room, picked up a book, and suddenly turned towards me. "What has your father decided to do, Maryam?" he asked.

"I don't know; but I think he's going to stay."

"Welcome. I'm going to stay too."

He strode out, and Fathiyya winked and smiled as she looked at his stooping back. Then he turned round again: "Why should I leave? If disaster falls, then welcome, things can't be worse than they are now."

When he disappeared down the corridor, Fathiyya said quite suddenly: "I'll marry you to my brother Fathi one day...he's looking for a bride. What do you think?"

"I told you I'm going to finish my studies."

She winked again, biting her lips, and said: "A likely story!"

My mother used to speak in the same vein. "If Fathi asks for your hand, I won't say 'all right.' I'll say 'welcome' just as his father always does." My father stood in the doorway. He was angry, something which was always shown in the way he trembled when he was at a loss to express himself. He shouted in his gruff husky voice: "Don't talk about marriage before our national cause has been decided." Whenever he expressed himself in terms of a cause, blood and danger seemed imminent. He had a special way of pronouncing the word "cause"; he'd fiercely stress the "c," forcing the word out. Hamid very probably adopted this habit from his father.

They'd picked his bloodied corpse up from the side of the road. I was standing at the entrance to the gate when one of the men asked me: "Are you Hamid?" Suddenly, I began to cry. My mother looked out of the window and broke down. Everywhere windows were abruptly opened and voices began wailing. The men silently climbed the stairs. He was wrapped in two coats, and one bare arm swung loose from his side. Maryam wasn't there. If she'd been there and seen him, she would have gone mad. Mother kept repeating this right up to the end. She'd sent me to wait for her at the top of the road and

I was to tell her to spend the night at our aunt's house. I was sent there too, while my mother stayed alone, surrounded by her weeping neighbors. Next day all Jaffa was in flames, and al-Manshiyya became a blackened heap over which bullets whistled ceaselessly. Then my aunt went and brought my mother to her house.

The lights were behind me now, receding into the white, silent horizon. On the other side of the hill I could hear the roar of trucks boring their passage through the night, an incessant drum of engines, but I was safely out of sight. The sand had given way to a rocky plain, and my steps quickened over this surer terrain. The wind was cool and exhilarating. I tried to look at my watch, but it was pitch black. As I did so, I came to realize how insignificant a watch is when compared to the absolutes of light and dark. In the infinite expanse of this desert night, my watch appeared to represent a temporal fetter which engendered terror and anxiety. Without hesitation I unstrapped it from my wrist and threw it away. I heard it hit the earth with a barely audible sound.

It began ticking in my depths with a sad abandoned sound like a small iron heart embodied in a giant. As his footsteps finally disappeared away from it, it began imploring for help, isolated as it was beneath the mad gyration of the studded black sky, as though anticipating an imminent mad attack. Then it, whose sole task in the universe was to guide, to instruct by its numerals, became lost in the face of that real time which had survived over eons without sound or motion.

I felt more at ease when I remained alone with the night. Without the contrived semblance of time, the barrier collapsed, and we became equals in the confrontation of a real and honorable struggle, with equal weapons. The black expanse before me was a series of steps no longer measured against the two small hands of a watch.

Its miniscule, tense and foolish time was spent. As it lay there on the cold pebbles, it seemed the only object in this universe existing outside real time. It was like a hornet, buzzing and circling madly round and round itself above an unfathomable river with no banks to bound it.

After a few steps I was struck by the feeling I'd cut off a part of my wrist. But I concentrated my mind on the transition, and so allowed my feet to move freely over the firm surface of the ground. It didn't take me long to reconcile myself to what I'd done, to feel convinced that no severance had occurred. Perhaps this was because I was going further and further away from the inaccessible place where it had happened. I'd done no more than scratch the dry scab of an old boil on my wrist, and feel the painful pleasure accompanying this, as a feeling of relief slowly pervades the body. And with it the memory of the wound itself disappears, and becomes as though it had never been. Nothing remains except a white patch that bears no relation to the wound that preceded it.

It wasn't long before the watch went crazy. Abandoned in its exile, it went on ticking to itself, building up that impenetrable barrier that madmen erect between themselves and the world.

He came calmly over and switched on the light. He sat down in the chair opposite and stared at me as though ready to embark on a long conversation; but he remained hesitant, drawing on his cigarette. The ticking of the clock relentlessly receded, as though the solitary stick had stumbled upon a new variation on the theme and was proceeding to try it out as it invariably did every time I left the room.

"Are you going to sit up and wait for him to get there?"

"It seems so."

"There doesn't seem to be any point in worrying yourself about his arrival. As far as you're concerned, he'll never arrive."

"Why's that?"

"Because you've no way of knowing whether he's got

there or not."

"But he promised me he'd write."

"What if he does?"

"What do you mean?"

"If he does write, the letter will take up to five days to get here. Don't you understand? I'll go through it more carefully. You'll never be sure he's arrived unless he writes to you, will you? Right. But there's a gap, because if he writes tomorrow morning, the letter will arrive five days later, and so, as far as you're concerned, he'll go on walking for those five days. And I don't believe he will write, because, when he left Gaza, he wanted to make a clean break with you and the past. So why should he write to you? If he never writes to you, then, as far as you're concerned, he'll never get there."

"Nonsense!"

"If you were to read tomorrow in the newspaper that an infiltrator had been killed at the borders..."

"Stop it!"

"We're just talking, aren't we? So why get angry? What I mean is, if something did happen to him and the newspapers reported it the next morning, then that would be..."

"I said, stop it!"

He fell silent for a time, while the determined, hollow, metallic chimes of the clock surged through the half-open door. I began counting them one after the other. Most probably, he was counting them too, for he sighed and spread out his hands, "It's eleven o'clock. He's still got twice the distance he's covered to cross, and we're sitting here like idiots." We can't do anything to help him or deter him. But what in the name of God does he think he's going to do in Jordan? Go to his mother! Ha!"

That was the first time there'd been news of my mother. I remembered the bitter wintry day that someone knocked on the door, and we opened to an old woman. She was wrapped in a faded blanket with rain splinters dripping from its hems. "Where's your aunt, Maryam?" she asked. I stood aside to let her enter, and once indoors she gave my aunt the news through her toothless jaws:

"Your sister Im Hamid's name was mentioned on the radio. She was asking about Hamid and you and Maryam, and wanted to know where you are." My aunt broke down crying, the tears furrowing the sandy fissures of her face that was lined from habitual weeping. Then as though to compensate, she began squeezing Hamid in her arms, hugging him, and imploring him to cry with her. But we decided to write to the radio station and ask for more information. Hamid remained adamant that the letter should be addressed to Im Hamid, although by way of compromise we agreed on different wording. Four days later we received a reply.

He sailed past me like a ghost and retired to his room. From there he called me to come to bed, but I didn't reply, and after a time he was silent. When I heard his heavy, regular breathing, I got up, switched off the light, and climbed into bed. But all the time I could hear *his* feet pounding on distant ground. At that moment he appeared distinct and tangible, and looked at me directly with his angry, despairing eyes that showed his deep isolation. He seemed alone and lost, perhaps abandoned. I went back to counting his footsteps while Zakaria sank into a deep sleep, his rough square face buried in the pillow. What in the name of God does he think he's going to do in Jordan? Is he going to cross the entire desert and bury himself in his mother's lap and cry? Poor overgrown child! For the past fifteen years he's lived his life without protection which he never dared seek, which he saved for fear that one day he'd meet with disaster. He's made his distant mother a refuge for the future, and he's been so concerned with developing that fiction that he's forgotten to nurture himself, a man who'd grow up independent of the need for her. Poor Hamid, what did you really believe? That the plough should remain forbidden to this fertile earth? That I should spend all the days of my life subservient to your manhood, conjuring out of your trousers a man from Jaffa called Fathi, who, silently and proudly, had been preparing a dowry worthy of Abu Hamid's daughter? You poor wretch! Jaffa and Fathi are both lost, forever—there's nothing left. It was you who placed that bier in front of me, to punctuate my days and nights remorselessly with this tragic truth. And it was you who introduced me to Zakaria. It was you who gave my mother an illusory existence. What do you think she'll say to you, this mother you never really knew. "Poor little Maryam, what sort of miserable life have you lived, that you've had to accept all this in the end? You were the flower of al-Manshiyya, ambitious, educated, from a good family. What misery made you accept Zakaria as a husband, with his children and a wife? My poor little darling..." What else did you think would happen when you decided, in one blazing moment, to leave everything and go to your mother? Perhaps you thought she'd come back with you to Gaza, that she'd walk into the house and throw Zakaria out in the street, and then restore Maryam to her old state of chastity and give her back the ambitions of her lost youth?

Without warning his legs collided with the foot of a small hill and he stood there trembling. This time his halt appeared to be decisive and final, and I could feel his feet firmly implanted in me like the inevictable roots of a tree. I was fully convinced he wouldn't turn back, but for a moment I also believed that he wouldn't go on, that he'd remain fixed here, pulsating alone under the naked sky until he expired on his feet like the small watch that he'd abandoned to run down of its own accord. The next instant, as though spurred on by his intense, solitary exile, the sky split open and a beam of purple light traced out an illusory waterfall beyond the horizon. Then, for the first time, I saw him. His face appeared rough, an impression heightened by the dusty color his short beard had acquired. His eyebrows formed a bridge above a pair of narrow black eyes. The short black hair that curled above his level forehead was dusted a brilliant silver. His coarse coat was the color and rough texture of canvas. His hands were big and solid, and the firmness of his youthful body, under his tight-fitting clothes, was taut like the body of a wild cat. He was deeply tanned, of that color acquired only by a body scorched for generations by the sun, passionate and warm, as though baked day after day in a mixture of blood and mud. For a short time the purple pillar of light remained suspended between the sky and the earth, then began to turn green. The distant sand dunes were altered in their turn, changing from brown to a dull yellow, while the black sky reasserted itself, fantailing from the horizon, and in its wake planting the flood of stars in their fixed positions. He realized that he had stood there and watched the sky open like a door.

What a fool you are to move on from one hell to another, to throw yourself up into the air like this. What do you really want your mother to say? It would have made better sense to slit her throat over your knees, throw him into hell, and wipe the blood on your face and on the walls of your house, and stay there. But you were too cowardly to do violence. No, not cowardly! It would have been futile, as ineffectual as your desire to place your mother between Maryam and yourself. To make your mother a wall of oblivion that blocks the past and to revert to some other catastrophe? In your mind your mother has always been an absent protectress, ready always to take up arms in your defense and remove obstacles that confronted you. You lived your whole life leaning on her. And what is it you want from this fictional support, that you, out of your failure and impotence, have transformed into a wooden horse? Why not sit down under this sky which reverts to its own depths and reflect on what you've done? Gaza's behind you now, erased by the universal blackness. The thread unraveled itself from the ball of wool, and you're no longer the person wound on to that spool for sixteen years. But who are you?

He suddenly dropped to his knees as though felled by an unseen blow. The rays of green light converged downwards on a single point in the sky, absorbing the momentary flash that had illuminated the pitch black. Outlined by that last ray of light, kneeling there, his hands folded on his thighs, he looked like someone that had been projected soundlessly into my depths, with the same dignified calm as the now vanished beam of light.

Are you sure she didn't get married, too? He shook his head violently as if to rid himself of an image that lived deep within him. How can you be sure she didn't marry as soon as you lost touch with her? In her letters she always stressed how she was living with her brother and his children, and taking care of them. You had no choice but to believe her. But how would you react if you were to enter her house and have her introduce you to her husband. "Once I was sure I'd lost everything, I had no choice but to marry." What will you do? Go back to Gaza? Visualise this and imagine her saying to you: "I still wasn't forty and I found myself totally alone. I had to choose between spending my life as a servant to your uncle and his children, or taking a husband who would at least buy me my shroud and my grave when I died. Hamid, my little boy! My poor boy! Did you have to come to terms with the world in this way?"

Couldn't you have found a guide or a weapon to take with you on this difficult journey? He seemed totally dejected and crushed, and he'd strayed a long way from the road. He wasn't conscious of how the night was slipping away. I wished I could say something to him, but I'm committed to silence. He was, no doubt, exhausted, thrown into this dark abyss, tortured and wounded, deprived of even a word.

Beating, beating. There's nothing left but this bitter wait, and there'll be no end to it—unless I should have news of him in the morning paper. Only then will I know that all is lost. I shall be left with Zakaria and the woman who carries his children, the woman who stands at the foot of the bed, staring at me naked in his arms, while I slake my thirst at her well, and lick his chest like a bitch. "Tell me Hamid, have you ever been with a woman?" At this question he looked at me abruptly, as though I'd slapped him. Perhaps he realized, unconsciously, that my contemplation of his naked torso (the lower part was wrapped in a towel) had provoked the sneering question. "What do you mean?" he asked, as he tied the towel around his waist. "Well, haven't you thought of getting married?" He shook his head by way of reply and said: "I'll only marry when I've seen my family brought back together in a proper house—not a hole like this." I walked around him and pursued him with my initial question: "You still haven't told me if you've ever slept with a woman?" Once again he looked at me with an air of astonishment and, perhaps for the first time in his life, gave me an appraising glance. Then, for something to do, he began to comb his coal-black hair. It was a thick crop and unruly. He never bothered with a mirror, because he knew he'd no sooner tried to make his hair manageable than it would go back to its old wild state. This had infuriated him once, but he seemed to have grown resigned to it now. That evening he came back late and, when he came into the room, he purposely made a noise to wake me up. When I opened my eyes, I saw he was still dressed. I knew instantly that he was, in his own naive way, intent on answering the question I'd thrown at him that morning. He began by searching for something he didn't want, then he turned to me and resumed the conversation, taking it up as though it had been broken off only a moment before. "I saw the blood pouring out of him with my own eyes. They carried him up the stairs bundled in two filthy coats. One bare, yellow arm hung loose between the men, and swung to and fro as though signaling me to join him. Crying out loud, I climbed the stairs, among the firm heavy footsteps of the men. You can say I've got too much imagination, but I've never forgotten that...and I'll tell you something else I've never confided to anyone...I remember one day rushing into their room, I can't recall why, but as soon as I opened the door and crossed the threshold I saw them together in bed. They must have been naked, but I only saw his bare brown arm circling her white waist. I closed my eyes, and turned on my heels and ran. The next day he came and sat me down in front of him and began talking. I can't recall what he said; but that's the only memory I've kept of my father. That's how I think of my father, just an arm, once embracing my mother and the other time bloodied in death. That's all my father means to me."

"He's young." That's what they all say, "He's young." But here you are, from the bravado of youth, isolated like a speck in the void, an air bubble floating invisibly with the wind's unpredictable flight. Perhaps it would be better to spend your life on your knees here, your forehead bent to the ground, waiting for some big foot to kick you; then you'll jump up, burning with shame. But here you'll miss even Salim's look which still burns in your guts. There could never be another whip to tear you as Salim's did through all those long, lonely years he's vacated. He stopped me one day, just a week after they'd entered Gaza, and linked his arm with mine: "Haven't you ever," he asked me, "wanted to fire a single shot?" Suddenly I began to tremble, as it struck me that this dangerous man was only a few inches away from me. But he showed no awareness of my trembling body and went on with his train of thought. "I know they killed your father," he said, "and no doubt you've been living with feelings of bitterness, vowing revenge and saying 'if only...'" He stopped speaking abruptly; his eyes narrowed and the smile vanished from his high cheekbones. "We have everything. Why don't you join us?" But the following day they ordered us into a single line behind the camp. Zakaria. Zakaria. Zakaria. I'd expected him to be exposed, but no one believed me. It was only when they led him away that I saw him, with my own eyes, take leave of Zakaria with a look of searing contempt. His face was scored with the indelible pride of a man who knows he'll die in public for a cause that commands respect. It was then that we stopped looking at him and turned our eyes on Zakaria instead. He was standing in front of us, his fingers twined together, staring at the ground. We stood in the rain, listening for the single shot that rang out behind us. Zakaria shook when he heard it, as though the bullet had hit him in the stomach, and he lurched slightly. We waited for him to fall; then we heard the second shot. As though by common consent our eyes spotlighted his solitary figure. There was a clattering of boots and the officer returned with a satisfied smile on his face. "Go home," he shouted at us. "You've seen enough." We slunk off, dejected, in the direction of the camp, each one of us carrying his personal shame.

He came home calm, and sat down biting his lips. He looked at me, then went to the kitchen and from there informed me, "They killed Salim and tomorrow it could be the turn of any one of us!" I followed him and watched as he filled the pitcher with water and drank straight from it. I noticed the whiteness of his face. After he'd finished drinking, he turned to me, and said: "It could be my turn tomorrow." I left the kitchen and went and stood by the window. I felt him behind me, and said: "Your turn? What do you mean? You haven't done anything wrong. They killed Salim because he's...well you don't need me to spell it out...but why should they kill you?"

She probably meant to reassure me. She didn't realize she was burdening me with more shame. I could hear her question reverberate: "Why should they kill you?"
Why kill an insignificant person, who could be left to carry on his meaningless life, to live and die cheaply right here?

With him heaped over me, it was as though the wind had dissolved him unawares. In time he'll whiten to a skeleton, dried up by the sun, immutably assimilated by the sand. He'll be like a sign pointing the direction to nowhere.

I searched the darkness yet again for the shape of the clock banging opposite me. Instinct told me it was close to midnight. I'd grown accustomed to the dark, which had now lightened to a mute grey tone through which I could vaguely discern two fine black lines against the clock's brilliant moon face. The pace of the hands quickened, anticipating the tumultuous moment of their union. I could hear Zakaria, sunk in his dreams, turn on to his side and begin snoring raucously. As well as I could, I focused my sight on the black hand crawling over the white clockface, and thought of the effort it expends all day for this transient meeting with the other pole that coldly awaits it, a meeting that allows no pause, only an instant moving on. If the two were to meet, embrace and then stop, they'd die. It was like all human desires that are spoiled by their fulfilment. The next moment the clock creaked and ceased ticking for a second, as though primed to announce a calamitous message to crowds waiting in silent anticipation. Then the big hand sprang to connect with the small one, and both were drowned in the metallic clamor of the twelve strokes. The last stroke came like the weary shudder which ends an orgasm. An instant later, the big hand slid off and resumed its solitary ticking pace in the darkness. Midnight. Dawn—that recurrence of light which threatens all fugitives—was just four hours away. Suddenly, it began throbbing in my womb: a slight movement that flowed through my body for the first time in some recess, unknown and infinite. That small stirring was like the tremor of a bird imprisoned within hands serenely closed. The movement was so slight I doubted whether it had actually happened, so I placed my hands over my womb; but there was only a silent and perhaps angry withdrawal. On a momentary impulse I called him Hamid, then took it back, and suddenly began to cry for no reason at all—or perhaps for everything for which I had no name.

I knew in advance what was going to happen. A small purple flare appeared from behind the hill, and ascended in nervous spurts, an arrowhead with a tail of blue sparks. Then, its initial rush expended, it exploded with a hollow sound and was transformed into a luminous purple cloud which remained sus-

pended, low down, at the end of a semi-arc of white smoke, traced out by the trajectory of the flare. The light turned hazy and embered into sparkling flashes. It had lit the ground suddenly, making it appear more mysterious than it really was, and totally unreal.

For the first time since I set out across the desert, an unparalleled feeling of terror gripped me. I could believe that the flat sand-hill in front of me, suddenly made distinct by the light, might conceal a demon, a man or a prophet, or some indefinably mysterious creature. I tried to calm my nerves, and to control the trembling in my thighs, which shook like an unruly animal. Bringing reason to bear, I told myself that one man or a group of men had fired the flare. The sure knowledge that I was utterly alone fired in me a fierce desire to fight in defense of my life, and all at once I grew calm and controlled the rhythm of my body and breath. I threw myself to the ground, moulding the shape of my body, as much as I could, to the sand. As I did so it occurred to me that if someone fires a flare-gun, it's because he wants to be found, and this made me realize that I was facing someone whose situation was the exact opposite of mine. For here I was pressing my body to the ground so as not to be discovered, while behind the hill was a man shooting a brilliant light into the sky so that he could be found. The likelihood was that we were both lost.

He knew nothing at all, but the obscure danger that had so suddenly surprised him woke all his instincts to action. He lay face down, clinging tightly to my breast. I felt his pulse beating into me, warm and steady, while the quiet relayed to him, from across an immeasurable distance, the sound of heavy steps being dragged over fine sand, from behind the hill.

All of a sudden my senses came alive. I began to measure the sound of the steps moving in my direction, slowly and cautiously. For the first time in my life I really felt the need of a weapon—here, where a person can't seize so much as a stick or a stone. The first thing I saw was a head appear at the top of the hill, blacker than the surrounding sky. The man hesitated for a moment, as though he too sensed danger, then, at a stoop, set about climbing the hill. When he reached the summit and stood there, he looked like the dark shadow cast by a stone statue, invested with a phantom spirit. He slithered down the slope, coming straight at me, and I held my breath, for fear even that would echo in the tense silence. My only weapon was the ability to take him by surprise, and this was enough to make me feel that I was being assisted by an invisible power. His footsteps grew distinctly louder. I guessed he must be armed, for a man alone in the desert who carries a flare-gun would certainly carry other weapons. Perhaps he was a soldier trained in the art of face-to-face combat. I felt that if he steered a course even two meters wide of me I would go undetected. But he appeared to be making straight for me, as if targeting me. Suddenly he was on me; I felt the ground hurl me up towards him and we fell together. I grabbed his upper arms, pressing my body over him, and at once I was sure I was the stronger of the two. Carefully and precisely I raised my knee and put it between his thighs. He began moaning faintly and said something I couldn't understand. Giving him no chance to reflect, I let go of one of his arms and threw sand in his face. This gave me the chance to search him thoroughly. I snatched hold of the small iron machine-gun hanging from his shoulder, and, I don't know why, threw it away. I took the flare-gun away from him, but kept hold of his long knife. He took a deep breath, but the shock had completely paralyzed him. He remained prostrate as before, and began repeating the same sentence over and over again. Then he sat up calmly and began wiping his eyes with his fingers, and spitting the sand out of his mouth. Once again he uttered a broken sentence, which sounded like an insult, so I told him to shut up. It was only then that, placing his hands wearily on the sand, he began to stare around him astounded. Then, with unbelievable speed, he sprang up, tightening his firm, slender hands around my neck; but when he felt the knife pressing against his stomach, he fell back and once again looked around him in perplexity. I realized that he hadn't in fact succumbed to my superior strength, but he had offered no resistance because he believed himself to be the victim of a mistake or a practical joke by friends; he'd never reckoned on suddenly hearing Arabic spoken in this remote place. He needed a long time to take it in, standing there and drumming his head against his thighs. At last he sat down with his head between his hands. I crouched next to him, gripping the hilt of the knife.

I'd grown used to waiting, so much so that I felt I could go to sleep now; but it was quite impossible. In my mind, I saw him as a child facing a strange, brutal world, a world like a small shattered toy, whose fragments were scattered over an area too wide for his arms to encompass. It was then that I decided to see her, next morning, before I did anything else. I'd knock on her door, and say: "I'm his second wife." It didn't matter how she'd react; only that I just wanted to meet her and see what she was like, and then I'd know how to handle myself with both of them. It seemed pointless just to sit and wait. I'd be denying myself life if I allowed him simply to use me as an alleyway between his school and her house, planting his sperm in me before he left. What an interminable, agonizing wait, Maryam, each time—and to end up simply as an alleyway! What a wait! His footsteps will resound on the wall all night as they pass over you, on the way from...on the way to...an ominous beating, beating, beating and time will trickle through your fingers like sand. Your long journey will end, finally, in this total banality. An alleyway! Everything you'd always hoped would be yours will pass you by without leaving so much as a trace.

They remained sitting in that vast, open space like two ghosts separated by a blade. They appeared unreal as they waited, with the icy wind of death circling around them, for the single moment of truth to come, an event that seemed as distant as their shoulders were close. Their coming together in that infinite expanse seemed partly an accident, partly an ineluctable decree of fate. They were so numbed by that they had to sit down together in order to absorb it.

At last I asked him, "Where have you come from?"

He raised his head, trying to penetrate the darkness, but he couldn't see the other man's features clearly, so he just muttered a single word and spat on the ground.

I nudged him with the point of the knife I held against his stomach, and asked him again: "Where have you come from?" He remained silent, calmly thinking, then he spread out his hands with a gesture of resignation, and shook his head. He muttered something and tried to stand up, but I forced him to sit down, and his air of helplessness returned. I tried to remain calm. "Is Dhahriyyah far from here?" I asked him, but he shrugged his shoulders and splayed his hands out in front of him. It was then that I remembered the incident of the flare. No doubt he assumed a patrol was somewhere near. At once I regretted throwing the machine-gun away, but I had no idea how to use it anyway—and perhaps it was better that way, because the thunderous noise, in this total silence, would have reached the edges of the desert. I was left with a hostage, with no idea where to take him or how to benefit from his presence. On reflection it might have been better to have killed him immediately, in our first short struggle, but this was impossible now, beyond my power, and utterly futile in any case. I could sense his nearness and could hear him breathing at my side. He sounded tired, lost and confused, but he was still alert, like a man waiting for something unexpected to spring out from between his feet. Suddenly the long night hours were taking on the slow unreality of a bad dream, a state of sleeplessness, a projection into a world of brutal nightmares. Once again I found myself facing a situation I couldn't cope with, a predicament which made me first smile, then suddenly burst out into laughter.

Zakaria turned over and looked at me. Then he went back to sleep, as though he too felt himself submerged in an insane dream.

"Perhaps you only know Hebrew, but that doesn't matter. But really, isn't it amazing that we should meet so dramatically here in this emptiness, and then find that we can't communicate?" He went on looking at me, his face dark and hesitant and somewhat suspicious, but there was no doubt he was afraid. As for me, I'd crossed the barrier of fear, and the emotions I was feeling were strange and inexplicable. "At any rate," I went on, "you can't remain an apparition for ever. We have to find you a name and a purpose. We've got plenty of time for that. By the time they find you with their dogs and their flares, we'll have finished creating you, and then killing you will have some sort of value. Only one of us can remain, you or I. The devil himself would find it hard to live with two illusions, to be trapped between the two halves of a press in which I'll be crushed.

"Let's start again. What's your name? It's pointless, I know; even if you could understand what I'm saying, you wouldn't tell the truth. We're going round in a vicious circle, and time can't work against both of us in the same way. They might be nearer to you than I think— but I'm closer to you than they realize. It comes down, as you can see, to a matter of distance, and perhaps of time too. But I'm not too worried about time, and as for the distance, it works to my advantage because you're nearer to the blade of my knife than I am to the muzzles of their rifles. There's another important fact you should take into account, and that's that killing you here, only a few paces away from them, maybe even at the edge of your camp, is a far more significant matter than being killed myself, because I'm a solitary unarmed enemy who's stormed his way into your stronghold. Everything's quite relative here and that's to my advantage too. There's something strange about that, because only a short time ago everything in the universe was completely against me. Everything that was happening, in Gaza or in Jordan, was working to my disadvantage, and I was rooted here, in this very spot, in the worst place I could be, surrounded by loss from all sides. So let me tell you something important. I've nothing to lose now, and you've therefore no chance of using me to your advantage."

If only I could make her understand I'm not against her and that she had nothing to do with what happened. But what use are words, now that I've actually become the second wife sitting in her husband's lap? Day and night I'll be the butt of the gossip of the neighborhood women. They'll say: "That's the slut who stole Fathiyya's husband. The poor woman's got five children by him; you can see them all there, running and playing in the sight of God and men." And you, what will you say? You, you, you, what will I mean to you, Zakaria? They'll say: "Her brother almost lost his mind and ran away in shame. She had her first child with him barely five months after marriage—what a scandal!" They can all go to hell, but you, you, what will you say to them? They'll also say: "He married her free of charge. She was fired up with youth and desire, and she's got a house with two rooms, two beds and a frying pan...He managed to chase away her younger brother, who's disappeared no one knows where." Liar! But you, what will you say, Zakaria? How will you stand up for me, now that I'm all alone and everyone's dropped away? What will you say?

The darkness was beginning to lift and a thin, steady line of grey haze straightened out on the horizon. The stars looked remote and less brilliant. The oppressive silence inspired in him a renewed sense of fear, and he began to look around him. Immobility had opened up a bottomless pit beneath him, and time had become his enemy. Hamid was motionless and seemed resolved on staying on this spot until the end. He was superior to his captive because, like me, he wasn't waiting for anything. To me he represented permanence and not transience. He, of course, was lost, but this meant nothing to him: not because he wasn't conscious of his predicament but because he no longer wanted to go anywhere. Since the advent of the night he'd been fiercely beleaguered, in this one remaining spot, until it had become his kingdom.

Suddenly I remembered him, and turned and said: "Do you know a man from Gaza called Salim?" He went on looking at the sand between his feet and said nothing. So I decided to give him a shock. "What's more," I said, "maybe you were the one who killed him. Anyway, we'll leave that for the light of day to reveal." Only then did he respond. He began talking without pause. He appeared both angry and nervous, flinging his arms around him, pointing sometimes in front of him, and sometimes behind. I prodded the tip of the knife into his stomach as a warning, and when he'd quietened down I said: "Don't use your voice to make up for that flare gun you lost. Anyway, I can't understand a word of what you're saying, so why waste your breath?"

The clock struck two, then fell silent for a second, before his solitary steps began to beat again in my head, and marked their time on the wall. You gave me this bier, you fixed it up opposite me, so that I can bury you in it; but it's your footsteps that will still circle it, and I'm the one who'll be buried in it. Even then your steps will continue to beat round and above it for ever. This small bier hanging above will, in time, contain us all. Your footsteps will drum on our coffin. Only you will remain on the outside, completing a journey without end. Or will it have an end? God! No one but you will ever know!

All of a sudden he took off his belt and began, with great care, to tie the other man's hands behind his back. He met no resistance. When he'd finished he went back to his place and sat down with the knife in his lap, burying his head between his hands. A cold wind began rolling off the hill, silently piercing his defenses, so that he pulled his legs up to his chest for protection. A muffled roar issued from the distance, and despite the approach of dawn the darkness still predominated. He stood up and searched the skyline for a sign; then, when he returned, he began turning out the other man's pockets.

When my fingers found his wallet, I pulled it out and examined its contents. Because of the darkness it was difficult to judge the value of the papers contained inside it, so I stuffed the whole wallet into my shirt pocket. He continued to stare distractedly, still hoping even now for a sudden miracle to occur, but at any moment, I was sure, he'd realize that the deliverance he was waiting for would mean his end the moment it arrived. I didn't know how he'd accept that realization, from which there was no escape. Suddenly he seemed to hear the roar in the distance, for he straightened up, staring first around him and then at me. Only then did I brandish the knife, to impress on him the kind of miracle he could expect, and he sat huddled again in his place. Next moment something startling happened. I was standing there, and he was huddled just at my feet, when I imagined in a blinding flash that everything in this silent desert, every grain of sand, every current of air, every star punctuating the map of darkness, was staring at us both with the same intensity with which we'd fixed our eyes on Zakaria, prostrate at the officer's feet, while awaiting the terrible moment of death. Salim had been standing with us in that unflinching row, his head buzzing like an irate bee hive, and before any of us knew what was happening, Zakaria was shouting: "I'll show you Salim!" Salim had spared him the full role of traitor by firmly stepping three paces forward and standing there. The desert exploded silently beneath his doomed feet, and the devastating years of silence rained down on me. "Why should they kill you?" Salim came and took me by the arm. "No doubt you've spent a lifetime hesitating, and saying 'if only!' Come with me now." His bare arm slid out and dangled beneath the two blood-sodden coats while the men were lifting him up the stairs. It swung to and fro as though inviting the watcher to follow. From the other side of the ruined wall we heard a single shot, and Zakaria keeled over, as though the bullet had been fired from our eyes which were silently fixed on him. Then Salim's mother came to me. "I went there at night," she said, "but I didn't find him. They've buried him in secret. Do you have any idea where? My son, my reason for living, all that was left to me." A half-capsized boat began battling on the surface of a black, flaming world. Where did they bury him? My mother had taken that secret with her and left us. It was all that was left to her. All that was left to all of you. All that was left to me. The balance sheet of remnants, the balance sheet of losses, the balance sheet of death. It's all that's left to me in the world—a passage of black sand, a ferry between two lost worlds; a tunnel blocked at both ends. All of it deferred, all of it irrevocably deferred. Then he slammed the door, took off his shoes and sat down as though he owned the house. Had I possessed a wooden hut and one square foot of land to call my own, I would have hanged him. But she never said a word; she let me go without a single word, without once calling out to me!

Without knowing why, I began to shake. I seemed to know, intuitively, that Hamid was in danger at that very moment; but if I'd wakened Zakaria and told him: "Something terrible has happened to Hamid at this very moment," he would have said I was mad. On impulse I got out of bed and felt my way to the kitchen. The silence squatted on the house and I could hear the steady ticking of the clock through the door. I drank some water, just for something to do, then opened the door a fraction and stared at the dark staircase. Then I went over to the window and looked out on the street. A quiet, deserted scene met my eye, glistening pale under the streetlights, and I returned to the kitchen. Again I felt it move with that tiny, jerky movement that was fleeting but unforgettable. I found myself standing up straight against the doorstop, and I called him Hamid.

I began to cry. A cold wind came through the open window and made me shiver. I went back across the room to find something to cover myself, and as I approached the bed I heard his heavy regular breathing. "Will he let me call the child Hamid?" I asked myself, and as I picked up a blanket, I wondered whether Hamid would allow Zakaria's son to bear his name. I went back to the kitchen and lit the gas, deciding to drink a cup of tea that would provide some warmth for me and the child. As I stared at the blazing blue flame, a new fury surged up into my mind. Why should I call him Hamid? Neither of them could stand the sight of the other. Hamid always referred to Zakaria as "the swine"; it was the only word he ever used. And Zakaria, for his part, always called him "the kid," for he could only see Hamid as someone who'd refused to confront life and manage his affairs. The two seemed incompatible, and the consequence of their meeting fatal. I remembered too that Zakaria had never wanted this child, a bundle of screaming hell that would turn me into a milk bottle, and that he was still hoping that I'd get rid of it in some way. O God, how can fate work things in such a terrible way? How can it? Hamid came up behind me in his usual quiet manner, sat down back to front on a chair and rested his arms on the back. "You make wonderful tea," he said. "Did you make some for me too?" I passed him his cup and he began sipping it, stinging himself with its scalding heat and smacking his lips. He'd come to say something after the days of embittered brooding. I didn't look at him directly; I wanted to leave him free to say what he wanted. He told me what was on his mind without any preliminaries: "Well...Can't you get rid of it in some way? Don't you realize you're carrying a bastard?" I didn't answer. He must have realized how fiercely he'd broached the subject, because he got up and faced me squarely. "I don't have any way of stopping this marriage," he said, "and the two of you have gone ahead with things against my wishes...but..." He paused again, walked away, and then said to me from behind my back: "Let me give you some solid advice. Do you really believe that a child who'll grow in the shadow of a man like Zakaria deserves to live?" He hesitated for a second, then added the insulting term I'd been expecting: "The man's a swine." I gritted my teeth and left. He followed me, pulling me by the arm, his voice rising. "It doesn't matter what I say, you'll marry him in a few hours. But even if you're prepared to destroy yourself and lose your husband, at least try not to lose the child...The only way for you not to lose it is to get rid of it now." He left me, slipped down the stairs and slammed the door angrily. All that's left. All that's finally left to all of you.

So what is there left for us and between us, you silent, angry apparition? My life and your death are intermeshed in a way neither of us can untwist. Who can know how things will finally be resolved?

A breeze sprang up, raising a whiplash of low, fine sand that cut their feet. Its sifting covered everything—the traces of footprints and the abandoned machine-gun. The breeze whistled as it raced southwards, reminding them both of my presence, that I was the ascendant force in their bitter wait. As the sibilance of wind carried into the darkness in a violent, cold, eddying motion, the two men became aware of that solid immensity of space that surrounded them on every side, that stretched further than they could imagine and deeper than they could calculate. Terror! The transparent air that carried a multitude of surprises, side by side. And the moods of my eternal body—love and hate and an unwillingness to forget. Time itself was rooted in my depths. Love and silence. Violence and anger. And before and above everything: submission.

I stood in front of the kitchen window, sipping the hot tea, as a broken cart trundled slowly along at the bottom of the road with a small donkey pulling it. The driver had fallen asleep and was swaying with the rhythm of the cart. The donkey followed a crooked course, sniffing the road and every so often finding something to eat. The two seemed, in their resigned journey, to be drifting over a hazardous current that threatened them both.

The clatter of the distant hooves became confused, in my mind, with the ticking of the clock on the far wall, as it described another circle. It too was sustained by a current that could neither be checked nor plumbed to its depths. Meanwhile Hamid was slipping away. For a moment I lost his features, and his face was a blank in my mind, just as his presence had dissolved when the door closed behind him and the sound of his footsteps receded on the stairs. He'd become part of that undertow which flows beneath our lives and which, unfelt, carries us minute by minute through those meaningless days which float on its surface—its power imperceptibly directing us towards an unknown future. It was then that I realized I'd been staring wide-eyed into the dark night since nightfall, carried undiscovered in his brawny arms, adrift like a sailor on a ship whose rudder has been smashed by the waves and must now explore strange worlds at the dictates of the current. It had been a terrible illusion to suppose that, when he really left, I'd ever sleep while his steps were imprinted on my eyes, night and day. "I'll write to you if I ever get there." But I knew that for an unknown period of time he'd remain suspended between me and his mother; perhaps forever. He'd step over our two bodies in that indeterminate world of time and distance that divides us by the gulf of the unknown. But for all that, he'd remain here as long as Zakaria's here. I could hear the sound of his scraping footsteps now, as though he was wearing shoes made of cork. He paused in the other room for a minute, then he came into the kitchen and stood behind me. "I thought you'd gone! What's wrong with you? You haven't slept a wink. What on earth's going on? Are you still thinking of the kid?"

"What's the time now?"

"I don't know. Do you think I watch the clock while I'm asleep?"

His movements were tentative; he came forward like someone checking out a place. Then he stopped and stared out of the window, first at the road, then at the black sky squatting above the low housetops and mud hovels opposite.

"It'll soon be dawn...What's happening to you?"

"I can't sleep, I can't...his footsteps fill my head, they never stop."

"Whose footsteps?"

"His footsteps, Hamid's. Have you forgotten him?"

"You're crazy. Are you listening to his footsteps?"

"I can hear them, I tell you. They keep pace with every beat of the clock. Hasn't it occurred to you that he...":

I broke off as I looked at him. He looked stiff and unapproachable, and appeared not to have seen the clock. I started looking out of the window again, but the hand he placed on my shoulder restrained me, and I was forced to turn around and face him. His tone was gentle, as though he was addressing a child: "Listen Maryam, if that damned clock's stopping you from sleeping, then I tell you what we'll do. You probably don't realize that if we tilt it a bit to the side its pendulum will stop."

He withdrew into silence, and a gulf of apprehension divided us like a wedge of iron—not a bridge or a wall, just a cold bar of iron suspended in the air. Night's talons had let go their hold on the roofs of the camp, and the sky began to lift slowly like a vast eagle at the instant of launching into flight. For a brief moment the entire future was contained in my mind in the form of a lightning flash that illuminates the enormity of the unknown. I began to shake. I felt his withdrawal to be undeniably harsh, and growing in proportion rather than diminishing. I waited. I waited. It was frightful for me that we both, standing there, should await his word, I and the child who was hidden, curled up in my womb. Without bothering to turn, he began to speak in a slow, subdued voice. I had to strain to hear his voice, which undulated between us, as though it was no more directed at me than at the objects surrounding us, vaguely awash in the lead-grey light. "A sixth child? A sixth! Can you imagine that? Do you expect me to jump with joy? He's the sixth child! I've told you often enough you should get rid of him, but you persist in thinking that he's something special to the world."

He broke off, as though he'd paused at a comma in a book he was slowly reading.

"And what do you think people will say? It's another scandal. A child after only five months of marriage!" He stood there angrily, striving to sort out his thoughts, laying out his reasons in jerky sentences. I was afraid he'd plunge into further complaints, but he carried on, obsessively, along the same lines. "Six mouths to feed and two women. I'd need a miracle to do it! You're all alike, you believe a child will tie a man for life, that this piece of flesh binds him to you. But, I tell you, you're wrong. A man with five children doesn't give a damn."

He turned around to face me. The dull light suspended at the edge of the sky behind him picked out his shoulders, and increased the darkness of his face. He took one step forward, then stopped.

"If only that damn kid, Hamid, was still here..."

Instinctively, as though prompted by an unseen force, I raised my hands and pressed my ears, then held them there with all the strength I possessed. His voice sank to a murmur.

He stood in front of me, waving his arms, expressing his various emotions of anger and sorrow. He brushed by me, his lips moving with increasing speed, while his voice crashed against the surrounding objects, rebounding noiselessly back to be sucked into that dolorous grey light that was like the surface of a dank marsh. Opposing him was another voice welling up in my body, echoing there, screaming into my head like the howling of a wounded dog that's had an empty metal drum put over it. "We can't dispose of him now, we can't get rid of him now." And as I stood there I realized clearly that I couldn't be rid of Zakaria now, any more than he could be free of me; all that was left to me was to spend the rest of my days with my hands blocking my ears and my teeth biting my lips. Hamid was receding further into the distance, his obstinate trekking steps pounding mercilessly on our foreheads. As we became intangibly united with the distance and there was nothing left but the echo of his stubborn footsteps, so he seemed to me to be like the last train that's left a deserted station, leaving us on its derelict platform, listening to that silence which belongs to places of exile and loneliness. Pounding, pounding, pounding.

The sudden burst of light made the sleeping desert, couched beneath the flat, endless dunes, seem more silent and expectant in its quiet. I could feel the blood coursing through my veins again. He'd sunk down at my side, exhausted, unable to prevent his nodding head collapsing on to his chest. Then he opened his eyes, drew a deep breath and tried to stand up; but he couldn't manage it. The realization made him look at me and, for the first time, attempt to speak. Coldly, I exchanged looks with him and began to pass the knife blade over the edge of my shoes. The sound of the blade emitted a drawn-out squeal. For a brief moment I was genuinely able to see him, and stare into the black depths of his glistening eyes, a dark increased by the flood of dull grey light that washed over us both; I was able to read in their expression a real fear and helpless, wretched expectation. Sensing my small victory, he closed his eyes, and when he opened them again it was to look at the ground behind me. He attempted to crawl on his backside, then he stretched out his head and said something, pointing to a metal flask two paces away from me that must have fallen from him in the thick of the struggle; but I didn't move. I spoke to him slowly with an effort to make him understand: "Die of thirst." But he continued to point his head in the direction of the metal flask, indicating by this that he was parched. I picked it up and tested it against my ear for the little it contained. Without opening it I threw it back into the sand. I looked at him, and at his parted lips trembling with impotent rage, and repeated my indictment: "You can die of thirst." Once again he attempted to reach the container by crawling on his backside, propelling himself forward by the heels of his boots. I allowed him to get near the flask, then yanked him back to his place by his collar. "You can die of thirst." Directly behind him the purple disc of the sun hung fire above the level horizon. A sudden wave of terror rippled over the sand, sweeping over us, and we both turned to stare at the water flask. Our eyes met again and the honey color of his became apparent. Lit up by the scorching rays of the sun, his face was like a sick man's. Downy stubble had grown on his chin and cheeks. The strong arms projecting from his shirtsleeves were covered with fair down.

While he returned my stare, I took his papers from my pocket, and endeavoured in vain to make sense of them. Then I examined the picture on his small identity card. He seemed younger in the photograph; his hair was parted on the side and his wild grin gave him a comic aspect. His name was written below the photograph in Hebrew. I pushed the card in front of his eyes, pointing to the place where his name was written, but he shook his head violently, pursing his lips. I smiled. "All right," I said, "keep it a secret." I went through the rest of his papers but found nothing of importance. Then I returned to his identity card, and in a small lilac stamp at the bottom, close to what was evidently something in Hebrew, I made out the word "Jaffa" written in distinct Latin letters. I folded the papers carefully and put them in my trouser pocket. Then I took up a new position and sat facing him. With slow, inexorable majesty the sun was already climbing the sky, although its heat was still subdued. The man looked at me cautiously and apprehensively, as though trying to work out my plan—but certainly he couldn't do that, because I was still unsure myself what I intended to do. I left him to study me until he'd concentrated all his attention on me, waiting for me to move or to say something; then I said to him: "Come on, be good and let's talk about Jaffa. This silent waiting's going to frighten us both to death." But he kept on staring at me with his tired, narrow eyes as though he understood nothing. "Come! How did it all end up in the part of the city that used to be between the mosque of Shaikh Hasan and the burnt Jewish baths in al-Manshiyya?" Suddenly, and without exactly knowing why, I sensed that he understood me completely, that he was following my words closely and waiting for the upshot of it all..."This could be an instructive conversation," I went on, "because I know that neighborhood very well. We used to live there." But the effort seemed futile, at any rate as far as he was concerned. All I intended to do was make it clear to him that there was nothing that merited his interest, that I wasn't harboring any concealed plan, and that if necessary we'd sit there until...until what?

In the distance a slight wind whistled, and began lifting the sand in an arrowhead racing towards us. When it reached us, it washed over us as a first wave of heat. He began to grow restless again. I stood up and scanned the four horizons that ringed us like walls. And yet that constriction was only an expanse of sand, a silent, far-flung waste absorbing the sun, the emptiness of the sky. Directly in front of us the sun's flaming disc appeared to be fixed to the height of a towering grey wall, and once more I sat down next to him and spread out my hands to indicate that there was nothing we could do. But instead of looking at my hands, he kept his eyes rigidly on the steel blade of the knife that lay between my feet and glittered in the light. I picked it up and once again rubbed the blade against the edge of my shoes, making it emit a warning squeal like a final wail. Only then did he look into my eyes, and once again, I glimpsed on his face that dumb air of impotent terror. Then I realized that it was in my power, at any moment, to slit his throat without a single tremor; and that, spurred on by the terrified gleam in his eyes, the squeal of the knifeblade against my shoes and the blazing sun mercilessly lashing the back of my neck, that moment would inevitably arrive. The range of sand beneath the high white ceiling, the sand range directly behind him, resembled a stage, where at the ringing of a bell, cars, dogs and armed men carrying black guns with tapered

muzzles would suddenly appear. But they would remain frozen in their onrush, realizing that they were in fact the audience standing before an empty stagedrop, and that the drama was unfolding before them.

He took me by the shoulders again and swung me around violently to face him. I kept my hands glued to my ears. Everything was silent, and I could see his lips moving vehemently in the tired, furious face he presented; but I couldn't hear a thing. He seemed to realize this, because he grabbed my wrists in his strong hands and wrenched my arms down to my sides. The roar of the world was reborn in my ears. Caught up in the confusion of noise, the clock hanging opposite the bed started to ring, its chime crossing the passage to the kitchen where we stood angrily, face to face, the morning after our wedding. I forgot to count the strokes, because they merged with his loud voice. The two together sounded like the clash of huge cymbals beating against my skull. "Do you think I married you to have a son, you rotten whore?"

Those sensitive folds of flesh that kept my eyes shut, burst open, and I felt the uninterrupted flow of tears stream down my cheeks. I tried to free my wrists from his iron grip, but he wouldn't relax his hold. The next instant a thin ray of sunlight entered through the window behind me, and falling on his face, split it in two, making his blazing anger appear still more violent.

"Listen to me and remember tomorrow what I'm saying now: If you can't abort that little bastard..."

Without warning I began to scream at the top of my voice, trying to drown him out with the unbearable volume. Yet I couldn't silence him and his voice exploded in my ear: "If you can't abort him then you're divorced...divorced...divorced. Do you hear? Divorced." My throat clammed up immediately and a bitter silence reigned in the room.

A dog started howling, and before long the noise was coming from all directions, an extended sequence of howls. Through it all I could hear a fiendish roar, but it was impossible to pinpoint the direction it came from...

Suddenly it moved for the third time. The tiny double movement inside me felt like a shudder, then it moved downwards to my thighs and knees. I closed my eyes for an instant. Then he started up again, mercilessly: "Did you hear what I said to you?" He shook me repeatedly, reiterating, "Tell me you've understood." Abruptly he pulled me to him then flung me towards the wall. Before he could turn round I'd crashed into it.

With its long glowing blade, the knife flashed in front of me...

There it is, on the table. I came bouncing off the wall towards it, like a rubber doll. My fists grabbed the knife, each hand pressing on the handle, tense and sure of purpose. We rushed together in a head-on confrontation, each looking the other straight in the eye. The blade projected from my tightly closed hands.

I felt it plunging into him as we collided together.

He gave out a long moan and tried to draw back, but the blade twitched again as he closed his hands over mine, convulsed around the handle. He closed his eyes. At that I let go of the handle and staggered back. The blade was buried deep in his groin above the thighs. He tried to pull it out, but his hands were shaking and turning blue, unable to grip the handle. He bent forward and leant his arms on the table. Blood was soaking his trousers, a deep red staining the insides of his legs. He opened his eyes feebly and looked at me. I turned round, took him by the shoulders and pushed him against the wall. His body remained partially upright, while his arms had fallen to his sides. He pressed his forehead against the wall, trying to keep the handle from making contact with it, but I gripped him by the shoulders; and, placing my knee against his back, I pushed him with all my strength against the wall. I heard the sound of the blade turning in him, together with the noise of the wooden handle as it scraped menacingly against the wall. He snorted as though awakening from sleep, and I could hear the blood hissing out in jets around the blade. Then he shuddered and collapsed heavily at the foot of the table. A narrow band of sunlight came through the window, lighting up a thin trail of blood that zigzagged across the brilliant white kitchen tiles.

Suddenly the silence reverberated, as dogs began to bark furiously and continuously

outside the window. They were only silenced by the sound of his footsteps, continuing above the noise of the bier hanging on the wall

and hammering with cruel persistence into my head. Remorseless. Pounding over him, and the bulk of his death heaped there. Pounding. Pounding. Pounding.

In My Funeral

My Dearest,

To tell the truth, I am not sure what I should write to you. All the words that a loving heart employs to express its separation, I wrote when I was there. But now, there's nothing I can repeat to your ears. What can I tell you? Should I impart to you what others would: that your love stampedes like a torrent through my blood? I would have been able to say this had the blood which flows in my veins been something of value. But the truth is that I am a sick man. The blood that burns in my veins is impotent; it is a substance that would become an old man, half dead, immobile, whose breast supports nothing but the closed chests of the past, and whose future is the guttering flame of an almost extinguished candle. And after that, an end.

I had believed, dearest one, that my wounds would heal with the passing of time; but the regularity with which I collapse tells me that I am like a vessel emptied of its contents, which can no longer remain stable. The passing of each new day digs deeper furrows into my resistance. The bitter truth slaps my face regularly, as a constant reminder. This morning I attempted to run up the stairs, only to feel my heart pull against my ribs and tighten, as if about to be severed from its veins. What kind of youth is mine? What value can be attached to it, my dear? And why should I carry on? What is this troubled specter which rises in a darkness blacker than a tyrant's conscience? What have I gained from this life of mine? Yes, what?

I had lived for a future devoid of fear. I used to go hungry in the hope of better days to come. I wanted so much to reach that day in the future, and the insignificance of my life was informed only by the profound hope that heaven was not boundless in its cruelty; and that the child on whose lips the smile of security had died one day would not spend his entire life scattered like an October cloud, grey like a valley riddled with mist, and lost like a sun which cannot break through the obscuring horizon.

Everything in life has proved contrary to a child's expectations. The years have passed slowly and painfully, and on growing up, his family demanded that he repay them for the support they had given him when he was too young to earn a living. Responsibility is in itself a good thing, but the man who endures an impossible obligation has his manhood eroded by the pressure it asserts. Everything presented an obstacle, and everyone he encountered contributed to his load and left him oppressed by a bitter feeling of inadequacy and unfulfillment.

Despite all this, I used to tell myself: 'Patience, boy! You are still on the threshold of life. Tomorrow, or in the near future, a new sun will rise. Aren't you struggling for the sake of that day? And when it arrives, you will be proud that you have built it with your own nails from the foundation to the top.'

That hope used to justify my daily pain. I would concentrate my eyes on the future, and endure the thorns of a dry road narrow as a cemetery path. Then something beautiful happened. A rift occurred in the packed clouds, and I was liberated from extreme poverty. Then I met you. Do you still remember? We met at a small party, and when my eyes first encountered yours, I felt the accumulated sufferings of my childhood disappear. Your hair was stormily dishevelled, and your eyes were lined with bewitching kohl. I found myself hypnotized by you. Later I read in your diary of your response to that moment, and how you welcomed me as a sailor about to pitch anchor in a harbor berth.

The more I saw you, the greater was my recognition of self-identity. I would stand before you like a child separated from the toy he coveted by the division of a shop window. Words would tremble in my throat, only to retreat unspoken. A drum would throb in my rib cage. Then I came to know you more clearly. You wrote in your diary about those days: "I am waiting to know him better..." At the time, I was still unable to write anything about you.

Then I came to love you with the resolution of one who seeks an anchorage, and with the throbbing of a heart that has suffered all its life, and with the strength of a man who has undergone vagrancy and privation just for this exultant moment of triumph. You were the lighthouse sighted by a lost boat. I held on to this discovery with the tenacity of one who longs for rest and tranquility.

You wrote to me then, saying: "Why do I miss you with this continual longing, if the word 'I' means us, we two, just as we had agreed?" I guarded my hope with the devotion it deserved. I wanted you, wanted you, with all the demands that word implies. Life had at last favored me, and that forbidding tower which stone by stone had obstructed my existence now afforded me its heights from which to contemplate my newly found happiness.

It was in another country that I earned my harsh subsistence, a place that had everything and nothing, that same country which gave you everything in order to deny you it. In that remote place even the sunsets were colored with a frightening deprivation, and the mornings brought the glare of remorseless anxiety. I lived there, nurtured by the hope that I would put all this behind me one day, and begin with you anew. But fate did not provide my sail with a propitious wind. When the doctor's eyes opened wide to inform me of the sickness in my blood, I felt the sails break up in my depths, and heard the sound of their collapse ring in my ears. The world spun with me, obscuring my eyes with a heat-haze. The doctor's eyes pronounced my foreshortened future, and the veins in his wide forehead were spelling out the arid, continuous torture to come.

After the initial shock, I heard the doctor articulating hollow, meaningless words about hope, courage, science and the compensation of youth. But words had ceased to have meaning; their letters had all turned into little worms recoiling around themselves incoherently. What was that courage the doctor demanded of me? To anticipate a future with the fatalism suitable to an old man who had transacted all his days in order to buy an afterlife like a merchant without capital? What was the hope when I was convinced of a prospectless horizon? What youth? Yes, what was the good of a youth that had never been kindled at all? That had never lived at all? What youth? How lacking in value words become when a doctor delivers a diagnosis!

But the worst blow was delivered as I came down the stairs from the surgery. I remembered you...and as your vivid face mirrored itself in my eyes, the fire of a raging black storm flickered in my heart. Would that lovely woman accept a sick man? I asked myself. To produce sick children? Would she wish to be my nurse? And to live with a dying man?

In the cruel days to come, I failed to project myself as the courageous hero the doctor intended. I felt that the small details which make up life had lost their importance to me, and that the future would be barren. I failed in my attempts at heroism; exhausted and depleted, life once again raised a tower in front of me like a huge wall of despair.

I am walking, in spite of myself, in my own funeral. All the hollow advice administered to me over the past years seems to have vaporized like soap bubbles. A person is courageous so long as he has no need for courage, but he collapses when the issue becomes real, and he is forced to understand courage as an act of "surrender," a detachment from human involvement, and is content himself with being a spectator rather than a participant in life.

On my way to my room, troubled by the suffering and dizziness, I felt you slipping away from that throne in my chest where you had lived ensconced, and through my fingers, and I knew then that I was entertaining a false hope of your surety. The sentence you had once written to me was ringing in my ears: "If your thoughts ever change, I shall leave you. The important thing is to realize that there will be a separation...do you understand the meaning of this terror?" But it wasn't my thoughts that changed, it was my blood, and with it, my life. I am afraid now to stand before you, begging your love, like someone who has lost everything. I am afraid—with all the meaning of this word—to look into your eyes and read in them pity mixed with rejection. I should then feel my foothold slide on the rock face, my life's effort recede, and that the valley beyond would never endow me with the least impetus to continue. Do you know what it means for a man to lose everything in the course of a short journey home? Can you realize what it is like for a young man to discover in a few moments that labors of his past have been futile? Then do you understand the meaning of a love that can no longer be sustained by pity?

I slept that night like someone whose boat is tested by a whirlpool. My head became a stage for farcical narratives that followed one after the other. My entire past was in need of revision. The values which I had upheld had, of necessity, to be destroyed. The dreams I had nurtured within me were no longer mine to possess, and everything of my past, present and future was coated with a viscosity that emitted a putrid smell. All the values that man establishes from conceit for his life on earth had turned into the hallucination of a drunk who seeks oblivion.

The confused ideas of a sick man's mind are a mixture of the comic and the tragic. For a few moments, I regarded myself as privileged amongst the thousands to be afflicted with a chronic illness. It seemed a unique evaluation, a rare medal to be worn as a decoration inside my chest, where I could hear it reverberate with the beating of my heart. But the truth was something else. And when I woke up, the full import of the tragedy faced me, morose, sharp and black, spanning my whole future to eternity, and smelling of impotence and privation.

Why was I thinking of you more than anything else? Everything seemed to me bearable, except you; you were the cause of my insistent suffering. Above all things I wanted to resolve the issue, to leave you and run away, or conversely to draw nearer to you, but my nervous stance oscillated between fear and hesitancy, the effects of which combined to crush me.

In a few days I reached a decision. I do not now know how I arrived at this conclusion; I have forgotten, or else events subsequent to it crowded it out of my memory. But what I do remember is that I resolved to become a hero for once in my life, to become one of the gallant whose names appear in stories as men who had faced crises with unsurpassable courage, and had fought back in the face of bitter fate. I told myself, happy I had at last reached a decision: 'I shall tell her the whole truth. She will know then the suffering I have endured in granting her leave to search for a happier future. And even if she does not understand the enormity of my sacrifice now, she will realize it in time to come. And anyhow, it matters little whether it occurs to her or not. What is paramount is that my conscience will have been set at rest, and my life will gain some tranquility and contentment.'

You cannot imagine, my dear, what this decision cost me. Let us say that I was a sick man on the verge of emotional collapse and could not fully grasp the act I was about to perform. I was in the position of one prepared from defiance to risk plunging to my neck in the mud; I could afford to lose everything, now I had lost what was most important. I wanted, I suppose, to divest myself of all moribund hopes, and this challenge was the only way in which I could prove to myself—even for a short time—that I was still able to behave like a normal human being. Whatever the motivation, my decision was final, and in journeying to you, the secret concealed in my chest, I could hear my heart beating loudly, and to no purpose.

What happened as a consequence, you know with the studied art of one who recognizes only one face of a coin and not the other. I struggled hard in my attempt to tell you, or to pant my decision, but the words remained locked inside. I was unable to stand, and adopt the stance of a Shakespearen hero, relating his tragedy with the daring approved of by the audiences. I kept looking for a rift to show, for a word to hang on to, for anything to support me. But my hesitation gave you the opportunity, the rare opportunity to demolish everything.

You were bolder than I and confessed that there was another man in your life, and that you were obliged to seize the opportunities which I could not grant you, but which he did. But did you really tell me there was another man? No, not by words, but through your eyes, the gestures you imparted, and the meaning behind your words. You indicated this with a frankness far clearer than words, and wounded me in this way before I could find the words to relate my tragedy and charge them with the condition of my illness. You said everything with the courage of a woman who wants to settle down. And then the door swallowed you, the days too, and you disappeared. It was obvious to me that you had suffered in our confrontation, but you left me with an unrelieved torment, facing the naked walls, and hurried away. You never heard the words I had formulated with such dignity, the words compounded out of my nightly contention with fear. The words I was denied the opportunity to speak.

My eyes remained riveted to the old door after you had closed it. I imagined you pounding the pavements of Damascus, and I could hear your every footstep. But you were at the bottom, at the end of the whirlpool, and I sensed immediately my irreparable, unfathomable loss. You do not know that you denied me the last opportunity to restore the humanity that I had been deprived of by this illness. You also took away from me the right to prove my courage. My life seemed an empty, meaningless shell, and it was as though everything bad in life had connived against me.

Why did you hurry to confess? Why I ask you? Why couldn't you allow me the opportunity to act out my last role? But you didn't know. Everything happened so quickly, and perhaps now you are in a park with him, laughing in his company, and speaking together about the children who will enrich your future. You both have the right to do this, but who can prevent me from feeling embittered, from hating you and everyone else, including myself? I could wish you all dead and every living creature too. Values and ideals? No, those are "your" values and ideals, those of you who have health and life. My values and ideals are something else, private and different, and attuned to the desperation of my life.

Do you see? The difference was that of a moment. Had you delayed your confession, everything would have been different. But the opportunity is lost now...and you have begun exactly where I have ended.

Kafr Al-Manjam

As soon as I walked through the door, I remembered just
how much I disliked this café, and how I'd resolved that morning to find an alternative place where I could pass an hour or
two. But out of habit I went in and headed towards my usual
corner where I could sit with my back to the wall. No sooner
had I sat down than my feelings of dislike for the place were ex-
punged by the realization that I hadn't brought a newspaper.
With my eyes I followed a girl who was wearing a tight dress,
and wondered whether my words earlier that morning had hurt
May.

As usual, the waiter pushed my cup of coffee in front of
me without my having asked for it, carelessly spilling the contents into the saucer. He made a gesture to take it back, but I told
him it didn't matter; it wasn't necessary to change the dirty
saucer, I said, because one's whole life was like that, with our
actions spilling into a grimy residue. As usual, he smiled without comprehension.

I was reflecting on how, outside the cracked glass window, the world was continuing with its noisy clamor, when
suddenly it happened. It was odd, that kind of clarity and sharpness. I was in the process of lifting one leg to place it over the
other, when I experienced a brilliant white sensation, accompanied by the premonition that something was going to happen to
me, soon. The impression was so forceful that for a short time
my leg remained suspended in the air. I quietly assured myself
that I was an inveterate fantasizer, yet the sensation persisted,
and alerted the nerves in my chest and eyes. I was positive that
this was happening to me for the first time in my life, but the
need to assert consciousness over the experience prevented me
from being overwhelmed by the occurrence. Automatically I
reached for my coffee cup, and had half lifted it when my hand,
as if informed by an invisible power, froze, and simultaneously

I saw the figure of my old friend Ibrahim materialize in the café door.

As he stood there, searching the tables with his eyes, I told myself that an absence of fifteen years had done little to alter his appearance. Even his movements were just as I remembered them, and for a moment I forgot that he'd been dead these fifteen years; this must, I felt, be someone who resembled him exactly. Seeing me, he nodded his head by way of recognition, then threaded his way through the tables, apologizing to those who were obliged to shift their chairs in order to let his huge body through. When he arrived at my corner, he pulled up a chair, and sat down heavily, without so much as shaking my hand. Then he looked around and asked for a cup of coffee. His keys jingled as he rummaged in his pockets, and, quite without warning, he asked me: "How are you?" I didn't answer; the event seemed so natural that I continued sipping my coffee as I looked through the cracked window at the road.

* * * * *

Ibrahim and I had been students together in the senior class in high school. Despite his apparent nonchalance, he was a sensitive youth, and intelligent to such a degree that our headmaster, in his weekly lectures, would single him out as an example of the perfect student. In fact, so outstanding was Ibrahim, that we regarded his success in the examination as a foregone conclusion, and even the brighter students tacitly acknowledged their own inferior qualities in the light of his genius. The news that he'd failed the examination struck us with the force of a thunderbolt.

Ibrahim disappeared the following day, and the last time we saw him he was standing in front of the notice board, but no one dared approach him. He must have read the results over and over again, slowly and painfully, his hands knotted behind his back, before he turned around without looking at us and walked off. The next day I was told that he'd committed suicide, and the newspapers confirmed this by publishing a report about his death. Apparently he'd borrowed a boat and disappeared at sea, and while the boat was retrieved, Ibrahim's body was never found. They also printed an old photograph of him, in which his hair was parted, and he was smiling.

But now, seated in front of me, he offered me a cigarette from his case and proceeded to light it for me with a gold lighter which matched his cufflinks. His cigarettes were a high quality brand, his suit was cut from the best cloth, and although he continued to observe me while I studied the signs of his wealth, he didn't seem embarrassed. I assumed he was accustomed to people admiring his possessions. When his coffee arrived, he took a long, pleasurable sip, smacked his lips and repeated his question: "How are you?"

Without thinking, I answered: "I'm bored." He shook his head, and, before taking another sip, said: "and what do you know of boredom?"

* * * * *

It was with a sense of agonized unreality that I read the names listed on the board for the hundredth time. I felt sure of one thing alone: that I no longer deserved to live. As I turned away from the board and walked homewards, my body ached all over with a dull pain. The world seemed to me to be chimerical, and while it appeared improper that I should live, I felt equally unworthy of death. It was then that I conceived the idea of hiring a boat, taking it out to the open sea, and there allowing the elements to desiccate my flesh, so that I'd die unnoticed by the living and uncounted by the dead. The man who hires out boats invited me to have a cup of coffee, and while we were sitting in his flimsy wooden hut, face to face, sipping black coffee among the torn nets, shells, boat boards and chains, he spoke to me of an unfulfilled dream that he'd nurtured for fifty years. Only recently had he realized that by continually reflecting on the multiple facets of the dream, he'd increased the unlikelihood of his

61

ever putting the plan into action. But, undiscouraged by this, he'd determined to find someone to enact the part he felt unable to play.

The man got up, lit the fire and busied himself with preparing another cup of coffee; and in that entrancing atmosphere, created, as I imagined, out of the continuous roar of the surf, with all its harsh, incessant monotony, I felt a gradual sense of drowsiness.

When the man returned with the coffee pot, he informed me that he'd give me a boat on condition I carried out his instructions. He told me, as he poured the black coffee into a small cup, that his elusive, miraculous dream could only be realized by someone who had no wish to live, and yet was unworthy of death.

*   *   *   *   *

I inherited this dilapidated wooden hut from an old fisherman I knew, on condition that I attended to his funeral arrangements at the time of his death. And together with the hut, I inherited the exhaustive dream which has continued to occupy me for more than fifty years.

That wise old fisherman told me of the existence of a city built like a fortress in the middle of the sea. Others had conferred with him about the reality of this place, which bore similarities to the fantastic cities of legend. Its walls are gold, its soil is gold, its pebbles are gold, everything associated with it is gold, but there's no shine to its texture, and the color's so distinctive that you wouldn't recognize it for the color you know as gold. But this is unimportant, for as soon as the traveler leaves the city, the substance takes on the same luster and the same carat value as the gold with which you're familiar.

The old man informed me that there was magic in connection with the place, and that no one found his way to the city without a special resolution. Also, should the person manifest fear, hesitancy or doubt, he would lose his direction and pass the city without ever seeing it. There were many who set out on the voyage and returned disappointed, because their resolve was inadequate to the task.

But the old fisherman would say that all was conjecture, for no one who went there ever returned to tell the truth. All that he would affirm was that he who was determined to get there would succeed, and likewise, should he be resolved to return, then he most surely would.

*　*　*　*　*

Kafr Al-Manjam!

As soon as I glimpsed it on the horizon, its name came instantly to mind, without my having heard the name or read it in any context. The passage was shorter than I'd anticipated. I perceived it in the distance and stopped rowing. I contemplated this black mountain in the vast expanse of blue sea, and felt a sense of awe as I progressed towards it, for despite its apparent darkness it glowed like a radiant mythic sun, and in its formation resembled a black woman squatting on the horizon. It was like being caught up in a story. As I steered my boat lightly over the waves, the ideas flooding my head found their echo in the roar of the surf. Before this, Kafr Al-Manjam had no existence on the illimitable chart of the sea, but now it was impossible to tell whether it had been disgorged from the bottom of the sea, or had fallen out of the sky—solidified volcanic lava or the meteoric offshoot of a burnt out star.

*　*　*　*　*

Kafr Al-Manjam afforded me entry, and inside that gigantic rock I selected a cave in which to make my home and began at once to fill my sacks with the copious gold that I'd find at the stretch of a hand, or could scratch out with my fingernails. And each time I peeled a gold leaf from the rock, another would grow in its place, before my eyes.

If the idea of living in a cave sounds unwelcoming to you, then remember that this particular one had walls of gold. Even after fifteen years I find it hard to adjust to the idea that I lived in a gold cave!

On my first night there I was aware of the enormity of my isolation. The solitude resounded in my ears like the neighing of a dying horse, but the glow of the cave's interior brought solace to the storm inside my heart. Intuitively, I sensed that there was something odd about the cave, and when I got up to feel the walls, my palms slid on a liquid oozing out of the pores of the heavy black stone. This salival moisture exudes from the walls every evening, but one soon gets used to it.

* * * * *

I got up and paid for our two coffees without his raising any objection. I glanced at him once more to convince myself that it was he who was sitting there, and walked out into the street.

It was a normal day; people jostled each other, cars competed for positions, and one could hear the curses of the cake seller. I told myself that I'd walk through the streets, climb the stairs to my room, open the door, throw off my shoes and fall asleep fully clothed, just as I always did.

Then it happened again. I had a sudden feeling of happiness. I put my hands in my pocket, and shook my head, smiling, as I quickened my pace. No, Ibrahim hasn't yet returned from Kafr Al-Manjam.

Beirut, 1963

The Shore

The young priest was about to proceed to his room when he caught sight of her peering through the church door, her eyes searching the wide hall, before she returned to her position at the head of the stone steps.

It was afternoon, and the shower had just rinsed the steps and washed the tiled roofs and given a radiant shine to the trees in the church garden. As a result of the rain, the town had taken on an oppressive atmosphere. Those who had contemplated going out to loiter in the streets or sit in cafés or visit friends had clearly preferred to stay inside. The rain had contrived to bring the day to a premature end, and there was a total absence of the passers-by who usually gathered at this hour in the main street on whose northern entrance the church was situated. The black asphalt mirrored the reflection of naked trees in large silver pools lining the sidewalks.

The priest walked between the pews to the outer door. He had just finished performing a marriage ceremony, and when the bride and groom and wedding guests had left the church, everything reverted to its customary silence. The deep feeling of sadness which had come to pervade him now weighed heavily on his chest. He had no wish to return to the book he had been reading before the couple had arrived. It was at that exact moment that he glimpsed her staring through a crack in the door, and then turning back to stand on top of the steps. She was wearing a light blue dress and had draped her neck and shoulders with a coarse white shawl. The sound of her shoes tapping on the steps made it obvious to the priest that she was wearing shoes that were too large for her feet. He didn't know why, but he sensed intuitively that she had borrowed them.

"Can I be of service to you, madam?"

The woman made no acknowledgement, and simultaneously he heard the echo of his voice and the returning desolation of the street atmosphere. What, he wondered, could bring a woman to visit a church alone at such an hour? The woman remained motionless, without turning round. In a low voice he repeated: "Can I help you in some way, madam?"

Very slowly she turned around and, as she faced him, he noticed the fatigue in her features. Her face, which was naturally wrinkled, had been made up with considerable finesse. The light blue dress was closed to the top of her neck, and the white shawl had fallen down on to her arms. In her emaciated hands she carried a small bouquet of white roses which she held to her breast. The priest felt that he was confronting a woman who had much to confess.

"I've worn this feast dress since Faris died," she said, in a low voice, like someone continuing an internal monologue.

"It's a beautiful dress, madam."

As the priest said this, he inserted his hands inside his sleeves, and closed his eyes. The woman continued to speak as if not hearing him: "And yet everything's over. It was finished before I arrived."

"What's finished, madam?"

She opened her lips to say something, then closed them stubbornly. Her eyes suddenly filled with tears, and, unable to overcome them, she made an enigmatic sign towards the inside of the church.

The priest shook his head and smiled encouragingly, then, with his mind full of many thoughts, he took a step down the wet flight of steps . His thoughts tended to distract his attention from the woman's speech and gestures, but he had decided in his mind to help her.

"No, madam, nothing's finished. The church is always here. No doubt you want to confess?"

The woman took a step backwards, as though she had been slapped unexpectedly. She pressed the bouquet of roses to her breast.

"Confess?" she said. "Why? I haven't come here to confess!"

She paused to look at the ground, then raised her head and looked into the priest's eyes: "No! Let other people confess, it's not up to me to do that! That isn't why I came!"

"Then why did you come?"

"I came to attend the wedding."

"I'm sorry, but you've missed the wedding by at least ten minutes. You're too late."

"No, I'm not late. I've inquired about the time of the wedding at least ten times, and I did my best to be here five minutes early. But you see, she got married without me being here, and I've missed the wedding yet again!"

The young priest raised his head to the grey sky, filling his lungs with fresh air, then looked down on the street stretching to infinity. He could see a little snow-white cat prevented from crossing the street to the other sidewalk by a puddle of water. So far it had managed to reach the edge of the puddle by jumping over a group of stones scattered here and there between the two pavements, and it now stood there craning its head, trying to discover the surrounding world. Each time it stretched out a paw to the water, it took a step backwards, contracted its muscles and began the attempt all over again.

"I could have come at any time. I've nothing else to do. I'm an old woman, and I've lived alone since Faris died. I was always waiting for this. I prepared my clothes last night; I aired them and then ironed them this morning. I was dressed before noon and stood in front of the window waiting, staring at the clock. Yet in spite of all the preparations..."

"Is she a relative of yours?"

"Who?"

"The bride?"

"No, no. She's not related to me. I've no relatives here at all. In fact, I don't even know her."

"You don't know her?"

Once again the snow-white cat turned, then reverted to its former position. The young priest wondered at the cat's behavior, trying to figure out what it would do next and why it wanted to cross the road.

It repeated the action of flicking out a paw, and drew back on contact with the water.

"This dress I got out of the chest last night is one that I haven't worn since Faris died. It was a gift from him. After he died, I swore I'd never wear it again. But somehow it's different now. You know, God shouldn't punish those who break their oath, because a person can't foresee what time has in store for him. But, here I am, late for the wedding in spite of everything. It's as if God wanted to punish me! As if..."

She looked disconsolately at the bouquet of roses in her hands and then held them up for the priest to see.

"And I've brought white roses for it! Can you imagine? I bought white roses! I went out early and combed through the market to find them. Can you imagine what I paid for a bouquet like that?"

He shook his head questioningly, noticing the tears that were coursing down her cheeks.

"I went without lunch for four days to buy these flowers. It seems wrong to attend a wedding without a bouquet. And now, you see what's happened. She got married ten minutes before I got here!"

The priest looked around, perplexed. He was confused by her narration, and unable to understand her predicament. He spoke kindly out of concern for her tears.

"You said you didn't know her?"

"No, I never knew her. I might have seen her once or twice at the most." The priest continued to stare at the road, while the cat still equivocated over how to cross. That white color, standing out in stark relief against the black background of the empty road, induced in him a feeling of poignancy and a bitter sense of loneliness and estrangement. The next moment, he discovered that the cat was intent on reaching the one dry spot in the street, which lay under a tree whose leaves had not yet all fallen.

68

"But if you don't know her, why do you wish to attend her wedding? And, why did you buy the roses?"

The woman dropped her arm to her side, and the bouquet hung there like something valueless and superfluous.

"She's a friend of my daughter's, a friend since childhood."

He expected her to enlarge on the subject, but she fell into silence and let the tears roll profusely down her cheeks. He tried to alleviate her suffering.

"Is there anything wrong with your daughter?"

"No, she's quite happily married."

"Thank God. Why are you crying then? If her husband's a good man, and if she's..."

"I don't know her husband. I've never met him."

"How's that?"

She looked at him, unable to restrain her tears. Then she turned her eyes on the upturned bouquet and began shaking her head: "She went away to Brazil five years ago, and got married there. I didn't attend her wedding, and so I haven't met her husband. Surely you can understand that. I brought her up just as God and her father and she herself wished, but when she got married, I wasn't there. She didn't even send me a wedding picture."

He was at a loss for what to say, seeing her standing there crying, shaking the white roses with one hand and wiping her tears with the edge of her shawl. After a while, he felt he had to say something.

"But she was a long way away."

"Yes, but what does distance matter? I'd been looking forward to her wedding day all my life. I dreamt of it so often. Watching her pass by me with her bridegroom. You know all those things... You know..."

"But doesn't she write to you?"

"Of course, once every six months. Young people today forget about their parents once they're married. Two weeks ago I learned accidentally that her friend was due to be married, and I also knew the time arranged for the wedding. Then I kept on asking about it to make sure I wouldn't miss it, but as you can see I'm ten minutes late, and I've missed the ceremony again."

"Again?"

She didn't hear him. She turned and started down the steps, her shoes sounding dully. "I thought she wanted to confess," the priest said to himself, as he watched her white hair. Black clouds had begun to build up behind the mountain, turbulent and quick, and he felt sure the rain was about to start again. Large drops were already falling and forming concentric circles in the puddles scattered by the sidewalk. He remembered the white cat and, when his eyes found it, he saw that it was ready to leap, forepaws extended, belly touching the ground, tail lashing the asphalt in readiness for the jump. Then it took a great leap, but couldn't outdistance the puddle and fell in the last quarter of it. It began to flail in the water, trying furiously to reach the other side. The dry spot was only a yard away, but to the cat in its desperate, wailing attempt to save itself from drowning, the place seemed impossible to reach.

At the same time, the thunder slammed in...

The Viper's Thirst

He'd been standing still when it rushed at him. It all happened so quickly; he'd wheeled around the instant he heard the screech, and suddenly, almost on him, was the forefront of a black car and a big wheel. And in that second he'd known that the car was the same one—it was the car itself. A purple cloud enveloped him, and he could feel the cold assertion of numbness in his extremities, heavy as lead, quivering like oil. People were hovering above him, they were dumb, and their movements resembled fish swimming around a glass water tank. He had been thrown prostrate over a jagged stone, and feeling its sharpness pierce his waist, he rolled on to his side. Drops of black oil were ribboning the asphalt, trickling towards a shiny red patch that stretched up to his cheeks.

The pain he was undergoing convinced him that the sharp stone was still lodged in his waist, but the corresponding sensation of numbness flooding his body brought him such relief that he wished only that the spectral figures would go away, leaving him alone in this hot place, observing the black tongue of oil as it crawled like a small viper toward the red lake.

A voice was buzzing incessantly in his head: "He was trying to cross the road and he was hit by a car." The voice was a familiar one. It could have been his father's, but despite its repetition of that single sentence, he couldn't identify the tone with any particular person. He couldn't even remember how his father spoke, and if his father knew that it was the car, if he only knew...what would he do? He assured himself that the words didn't come from his father, for if he was here, he would hardly be sitting there saying over and over again: "A car hit him."

He was still enjoying the delicious sense of numbness that suffused his body, and although he could feel hands carrying him, examining him, pressing parts of his body, they could not detract from the pleasure he derived at being dissociated from their touch.

"Can you count my fingers?" The voice he heard seemed to be speaking into cotton. His ears vibrated as they caught the sound, turning it over and then thrusting it to the back of his head. It wasn't his father's voice; it must be the voice of cotton. When his father spoke, it was with the resonance of bronze, a loud voice that shook the roof of their old house, so that his mother was prompted to say: "If your urge to work was as strong as your voice, we'd have a good life!"

How could he have thought to forget his father's voice? It was impossible. Had he not heard it year after year, as he walked beside him along those alleys paved with smooth, curved stones? And on what did his father use to discourse? He was too confused to remember, it would all come back later; for the present there was only the sensation of numbness, a delicious heaviness coursing his veins.

"If you can count my fingers, tell me how many there are, and if you can't see them, then tell me that too. Can you hear me?" He used to hear his father's voice in the adjoining room; he would be telling his mother: "They'll marry Laila to Abd el Hadi. Don't you know who Abd el Hadi is? He's the son of Hasan who died, and used to live above the grocer's."

And his mother, busy picking little stones from a plate of uncooked rice, would ask: "When's the wedding?"

"Tonight," would be the affirmative response from the bronze voice in the adjoining room.

Tonight ! He would be waiting for this wonderful word, with all the mysterious connotations it implied. And at once, he would get up and climb the ladder to the attic. There he always found the long stick quickly, but failed to discover the little drum. He would shout down the stairs: "Where did you put the drum? It's not here!"

And in response to his question, he'd hear his father's angry voice enjoining him to come down: "Come down here, you imp. When will you ever learn that the drum's kept in the courtyard and not in the attic? We've told you a thousand times, but you never seem to take it in."

As he climbed down the ladder he would recall how his father had once told him that the drums should never be kept in a damp place, but should be stored where there was access to sunlight, in order to ensure that the drumskins remained taut.

"My dear child," the voice was saying, "just tell me if you can see my hand?" His father's hand was tough, large and wide, with blue pulsing veins that protruded from the skin. He would turn the drum over in his hands and then tap it with his index finger. He himself would be squatting opposite him, observing each movement and allowing nothing to escape his attention. He would watch his father put on baggy trousers that were embroidered at the sides, immediately below the pockets, and then pull on his shiny striped vest with its row of small black buttons, wrap a long black belt around his waist and tie its ends so that the knot wouldn't show. Only after this preparation was complete would he stand up and ask: "Can I come with you tonight, father?"

And without so much as glancing at him, his father would answer: "Yes, by all means come with me, but you must learn, not just watch."

Then kneeling down in front of him in order to grip his small arms, he would say: "Tell me, if I was to die tomorrow, who would you learn this skill from? And what would your future be? Tonight pay special attention to how I do things. You have to learn someday!"

But he never did learn. He must have seen his father on countless occasions walking at the head of the wedding procession, while he kept pace at his side, observing his hands and his steps, but taking nothing in. Everything about the procession was so complex that he couldn't imagine how he would ever learn the technique of drumming. He would never be able to deal out those quick masterful blows on the small drum, with such finesse. His eyes couldn't follow his father's hand as it passed the drum behind his back, through his legs, and then behind his neck, while, at the same time, the cane never ceased striking the drum with those astonishing blows, and his father continued to sing in an unwavering voice throughout the duration of the swift, marvelous dance.

The voice was coming at him again. "We want to treat you, my boy...why don't you answer my questions? I'm not going to hurt you. Just tell me if you can see my hand, and shake your head... Try to answer...do you see it?"

But he never did learn. He had tried so many times to make those same movements in front of his father, and his failure had brought him close to tears. Once when he had tried to revolve the drum behind his back, it fell from his hands and he had failed to catch it. He had run to the next room and started wailing, only to hear his father say to his mother: "The boy must be stupid. It's his father's skill and his grandfather's before that, so how can he be this untalented? Here I am, an old man on the verge of death, and your son still hasn't learnt how not to let the drum fall out of his hand!"

Despite these incidents, he was exceedingly happy. He would watch his father's hands at work in every ceremony, and imagine that the motions were performed by some kind of inimitable magic. In his neighborhood, he felt proud of being the son of the man who was esteemed at every wedding, and around whom the young men in the procession would gather as they escorted the bridegroom to the bride's house, clapping and singing along with him, and extolling his virtues as a drummer. How he could beat the drum from the hollow of his back, from behind his neck, from between his legs, with the stick never once missing the drum, and its strokes timed with perfect precision!

"You try to reach him," the voice said. "I have a thousand patients to see, he's not the only casualty in this hospital."

He felt a soft hand wiping his brow and a woman's voice reached him from a distance, as though her words were wrapped in cotton wool. "Why don't you want to cooperate?" the voice said. "Can you see my face?"

He could hear his father again talking to his mother in the adjoining room. "They say that cars are better. Imagine! Since Abd al-Muhsin got married five months ago, the talk in the café has centered around the notion that cars are better than wedding processions. And have you heard the cars croaking like frogs as they carry people packed into them like sardines? It's a crying shame. People get married without a procession as though they were ashamed of marriage. Today the café owner told me to look for another job."

That day, the brooding atmosphere told him that something really bad had happened, so he got out of bed and crept to the door. He saw his father sitting crosslegged on the mat, while his mother oiled the drumskin. He heard his father go on: "I had imagined that the other neighborhoods had stopped inviting me to their weddings because of a rival, but in fact it's all to do with cars. My God! Imagine the bridegroom cowering in a car as if he were ashamed to be seen. It's a disgrace. The most joyful day of one's life! A few blasts on some car horns, and it's all over!"

He had returned quietly to bed, and all night dreamt of cars carrying the bride and bridegroom without the benefit of drum and stick. "Listen!" the voice was saying, "we'll throw you out in the street if you won't talk. What a confounded brat. He opens his eyes like a cat and looks at us without saying a word. Who's your father?"

His father? He'd gone out one day and not returned. A neighbor, the carpenter, Muhammad Ali, was marrying off his son, and his father had prepared the drum for the ceremony. In the afternoon he'd told his mother that Muhammad Ali hadn't invited him to the wedding. When the cars arrived in the evening, their horns blaring and their bodywork shining as if newly polished, his father had gone out into the street. He had tried to follow him but he had been prevented from doing so by his mother. He had heard a clamor and then an ugly altercation. His mother was staring from a crack in the window, and prevented him from seeing what was happening, so he crept to the door and opened it noiselessly. When he peered out he saw the shiny forefront of a black car and a big wheel. It was parked directly in front of the door. When he put his head out further, he was in time to see a large stone smash the car windows. By now the clamor had increased, so he closed the door and retraced his footsteps.

In the morning he heard his mother talking to a visitor in subdued tones. She was evidently speaking of his father, and he could hear her say: "He began throwing stones at the wedding car, and then lashed out with his stick. Muhammad Ali called the police after he almost killed the driver with it."

The voice was returning again: "He has a serious injury to his waist, but the important thing is to discover the condition of his eyes. There's also a head wound. But is he ever going to be able to talk?"

Once again he felt the soft hand on his forehead and he heard the woman's voice: "Did you see the car that hit you, my dear?"

It was the car itself, the same car—the black shiny one that had the gloss of oil, and a huge tire of furrowed rubber. He was quite sure of that; it had followed him ever since the incident in which his father had thrown stones at it, and eventually it had hit him. 'But why had it done that?' he asked himself. He hadn't been a party to his father's actions, and he'd been walking on the pavement in apparent safety.

"Tell us, my dear, did you see the car that hit you? If so, then just nod your head."

If his father was informed of what had happened, he would smash the car. But what was the use now? They would never know that the car had intended to hit him, and had mounted the pavement in order to do so. And if his father really was here, would he be standing with those who asked him to count their fingers? Would he waste his time on such trivialities?

"What's your name? What's your father's name? Where do you live? Try and tell us..."

But it was no use; he lacked the ability to learn. Once when he dropped the drum it almost broke. It was stored in the

76

attic now. His mother had removed it from the courtyard, and his father had never returned.

"Why don't you try to cooperate? Why won't you speak?" The voice had found him again.

He would have liked to help them, but he was unwilling to relinquish the sense of euphoric numbness that coursed sluggishly through his veins. How terrifying it all seemed! He had been lying there, a sharp stone penetrating his side, and when he'd turned over, he'd seen drops of black oil dripping from the front of the car, then trickling with slow deliberation towards the small pool of blood that stretched up to his nose. He had closed his eyes to shut out the image of a black viper crawling to drink from the red pool.

"Leave him," the voice said. "Perhaps he needs to rest for a while. We'll come back later."

The black viper advanced, slow, cruel, repulsive, then plunged into the small pool of blood and began to lick the red liquid with a long, thin tongue.

The Cake Vendor

Was it simply a coincidence that I should meet him again, in the same place where I first encountered him?

He was squatting there as if he'd never once shifted his position, with his rough black hair, his eyes lit up with a dull gleam of hopelessness, hunched over his wooden box, and staring at the shine of an expensive pair of shoes. For an entire year his image had remained constant with me, indelibly engraved on my mind, ever since I'd first seen him in that particular corner. And for no apparent reason, other than that I myself had occupied this same spot ten years earlier, when I was passing a most difficult period of my life. My way of polishing shoes had been similar to his; my vision of the whole universe was a shoe—its toe and heel represented two cold poles between which my entire world was contained.

When I'd first seen him, a year earlier, his mouth had spat out a mechanical offer without even looking at my shoes. "I can make them shine like a mirror, sir," he'd hurriedly affirmed.

Motivated by the desire to find compensation for the long months of suffering, I placed a foot squarely on the hump of the box, and looked at the broad line of sweat rimming his dirty blue shirt. His small, thin shoulder muscles began to expand and contract, while his head nodded rhythmically.

"These are cheap shoes," he'd commented.

I didn't feel insulted, for my feelings on seeing a cheap pair of shoes had been similar to his, except that I'd refrained from expressing myself so naively. Cheap shoes gave me the feeling of being close to the world, but I had no intention of discoursing on that topic.

"How old are you?" I asked.

"Eleven."

"Palestinian?" I questioned.

His answer came by way of a wordless nod, and I sensed in that gesture an element of concealed shame.

"Where do you live?" I enquired.

"In the refugee camp," he responded.

"With your father?" I ventured.

"No, with my mother," he said.

"You go to school, don't you?" I continued.

"Yes," was his terse reply.

He flicked his thumb against the sole, looked up at me with two limpid eyes, and stretched out his small palm in my direction. I experienced a moment of anguish, and the realization of two conflicting emotions struggling for ascendancy within me. Should I give him his normal rate, or should I offer more? When I received my minimum fee, I'd feel pride at the dignity of my work, and when I was tipped, a sense of humiliation would overshadow my happiness at the extra money I earned. I could feel his eyes burning my back as I turned the corner, after having paid him no more than his due. When I looked round, he'd averted his eyes, and was once more staring at the pavement in the hope of detaining another passerby.

However, my association with Hamid didn't end here, for less than a month later I was appointed to the position of teacher in one of the refugee schools, and on entering the classroom for the first time I found him sitting in the front row. His rough black hair was shorter than before, his threadbare shirt was inadequate to cover his nakedness, and his eyes still bore traces of an inerasable sadness.

I was pleased when he didn't acknowledge me, and though it seemed natural that a shoe-shine boy should forget his casual customers, I was still obsessed with the fear that he'd recognize me. Had he done so, then my presence in the class would have been constantly overshadowed by a feeling of embarrassment. Throughout my first lesson I tried unsuccessfully to distract myself from his face, which combined an expression of attentiveness with visible anxiety. The class itself was made up of others like Hamid, children waiting impatiently for the final bell to sound, when they'd take off through the alleys of Damascus, racing against dusk to earn their supper. They awaited the hour of their liberty with impatience, fanning out under the cold, grey sky, each of them pursuing their own course in life, and as night fell, they would return to their tents or mud huts where a family remained crammed together, silent the whole night through, except for the sound of suppressed coughing.

I used to feel that I was teaching children who were old for their years. The spark in each of them seemed to have been ignited by the harsh friction of contact with a rough edged life. In class, the movement of their eyes seemed like the reflection of small windows looking out from mysterious, dark planets. They kept their lips firmly closed, as though they feared to let loose the string of curses that would otherwise issue from them. The class was a miniature world, a microcosm full of misery of a heroic kind. I felt alien to their shared characteristics, a feeling that made me only the more determined to get to their feelings and thoughts.

Hamid was of average intelligence, but he showed no inclination to study, and my efforts to encourage him were to no avail.

"Hamid," I'd say, "don't pretend to me that you study at home, because I know you never do."

"No, sir."

"Why don't you study?" I continued.

"Because I work," was his reply.

"Till what hour?" I asked.

He looked up with big, sad eyes, while his small fingers nervously twirled a dirty cap, and whispered in a despondent voice: "Until midnight...sir... The people leaving the cinema always buy my cakes if I wait outside for them."

"Cakes? So you sell cakes?" I said, somewhat incredulously.

"Yes, sir... cakes," he answered bashfully.

"I thought you... Never mind, go back to your seat."

Throughout the night I was plagued by the recurrent image of that poor little boy wandering barefoot through the streets of Damascus, and waiting for the cinema audiences to decamp into the street. It was a rainy October night. I imagined him standing on a corner trembling like a leaf in a storm, his shoulders hunched, his hands pressed into the rents in his clothes. He'd be staring at the tray of cakes in front of him, anticipating a hungry customer who'd buy a cake from him, or perhaps two customers...or three...his lips framing a hopeless smile, before he resumed staring at the swirling October gutters.

The following day I saw him in class. His eyes were heavy with sleep, and periodically his head would abruptly nod on to his chest, only to be wearily retrieved.

"Do you want to sleep, Hamid?" I asked.

"No, sir," was his reply.

"If you want to sleep, I can take you to the teacher's room."

"No, sir."

Nevertheless, as he appeared especially fatigued, I led him off to the privacy of the teacher's room. It was bare except for a single picture executed by the unsuccessful drawing master with the remnants of the students' paint. Heavy chairs were scattered along the damp walls and round a table piled high with books and students' papers. Hamid stood uncertainly in the doorway. He was clearly anxious, and he twirled his cap with his fingers. He looked alternately at me and then at the room.

"Sleep on any chair you like," I said. "We'll put some firewood in the stove."

He moved towards the nearest chair and half sat on it, his eyes shining with the gratification of being warm.

"Did you sell any cakes yesterday?" I enquired.

"Not many," he replied dejectedly, and I noticed that his face trembled.

"Why?" I asked.

"Because I slept," was the reply. "I fell asleep while I was waiting for the film to end, and when I woke, everything was already over."

"Sleep now," I said. "I'll go back to the class."

I don't know how I completed the lesson. The emotions welling up in me were such that I felt I might burst into tears in front of the students.

During the break, I found Hamid fast asleep. His nose was still blue from cold, but color was coming back to his cheeks. None of the staff asked questions, as incidents like these were commonplace, and everyone was only too happy to sip his tea in silence.

In the course of the next few days I tried to think of a way to enter Hamid's life without arousing his curiosity. This was no easy accomplishment as every student in the refugee school insisted on preserving his own sense of individuality, holding on to it as a lifeline, as if there was an unspoken agreement that this was both necessary and a duty. When they occur at the right time, small incidents take on a significance beyond their actual size: that is to say, every major event is possessed of a small beginning. One day my younger brother came to school bringing me my lunch. When I was informed of that, by one of the school servants, I sent Hamid to collect it. When he returned I sensed that he'd been insulted in one way or another. As a consequence I asked him to come to the teacher's room during the lunch break.

Despite the fact that I was alone, he entered the room with his customary sense of anxiety. His fingers worked agitatedly at his cap, and his eyes gleamed with characteristic ferocity.

"Hamid," I said, "did you like my brother?"

"He's like mine," he said.

I hadn't imagined that the subject would be broached so quickly, and so it was that I asked him in surprise: "Your brother? I thought you only had sisters."

"Yes," he said, "but my brother died."

"Died?"

I felt an increasing sense of frustration at this young-ster's trait of secrecy.

"Was he younger than you then?" I asked.

"No, older."

"How did he die?" I questioned.

Hamid didn't answer. I saw him fight to hold back tears that overcame him in the end; trickling rivulets that he furtively tried to conceal.

"Don't speak..." I told him. "If it's any consolation, you may like to know that I too had a brother who died."

"Really?"

"Yes...a big car ran him over," I added.

I was lying, but I wanted to sympathize with the boy's sorrow in some way. I felt that my lie had gone straight to his heart, for his eyes were suddenly expressive of a new sorrow, and he continued talking slowly: "My brother wasn't run over by a car. He was working as a servant on the fourth floor of a building at the time, and he was quite happy."

Hamid was using his arms to clarify his meaning and was unconscious of the tears streaming down his face.

"He put his head out of the lift while it was coming down, and his head was cut off."

"He died?"

It was a stupid question, but an involuntary one, aimed at allaying the sudden fear that gripped my body. Hamid nodded his head and asked: "Did the car cut off your brother's head?"

"My brother? Oh! yes...yes it did!"

"Did you mourn over him a lot?" Hamid continued.

"Yes."

"Do you cry when you remember him?"

"Not much," I admitted.

"Tell me, sir," he questioned, "do you have a father?"

"Of course. I mean, yes, why?"

He took one step forward and asked me with tremulous eagerness: "Is he well?"

"Yes." I said. "Why?"

After that, Hamid seemed to withdraw. His eyes receded into their sockets, and I could sense a tentacular pressure squeezing his lungs. He tightened his lips, and I knew that any attempt to question him would be futile. He stared blankly at the bare wall. His pants were short and torn, and his blue shirt was dirty and frayed. He collected himself and blushed when he realized that I'd been watching him in his state of confusion. He twirled his woolen cap even faster between his fingers.

After that, the problem of Hamid began to infiltrate my life. I found it hard to be the detached observer of his tragic life, and from all of the shared poverty of the class, it was Hamid's sad predicament and the desperation in his eyes that attracted me. I thought of him constantly. I contemplated going beyond the bounds of duty, and investigating his life systematically. It even occurred to me that I might be able, indirectly, to help him financially, but in a way that would involve no sense of humiliation on his part. But I'd have to proceed with caution or else meet with failure, for in his eyes I discerned not only sorrow but also a great deal of pride and dignity.

However, a series of small incidents led to a diminution of my involvement with Hamid's case. Indeed, I bore a strange grudge against this hungry, complicated young creature whose many secrets led to his problems remaining permanently unresolved. It happened that one day he complained to me of a teacher colleague who'd grievously insulted him. Staring at me, and scowling surlily, Hamid said: "If I wasn't an orphan I'd have called my father."

"Eh...your father's dead?" I asked sharply.

He shyly lowered his head and said:

"Yes."

"Why didn't you tell me before?" I questioned.

Instead of answering, he nodded his head continuously and remained silent.

"Then it's left to you to support your family?" I enquired.

"Yes," he replied, "it's up to me. My mother earns a little cleaning the stores of the relief agency, but I earn more."

He lapsed into silence again, then, spreading out his small hands expressively, he said with vehemence: "I buy three cakes for ten cents and sell each one for five."

"Do you still fall asleep while you're waiting for the crowds to come out of the cinema?" I asked.

"No," he replied, "I'm used to late nights now."

If the truth were known, I suppose every teacher would have to confess to having cheated in order to assist an unfortunate student to succeed. I myself used to do it. Despite his being of ordinary intelligence, Hamid's marks were always good, and I never felt the fairness of my marking system to be clearer than in Hamid's case. But it wasn't at this stage that the issue became complicated. It grew to be so only when I started to have doubts about Hamid's behavior, and the things he told me, and the authenticity of his tears.

The whole thing dated from a scorchingly hot day at the end of the school year. The students relayed to me that one of the school servants had severely beaten Hamid as he tried to break out of the school compound. When I summoned the servant to the teacher's room with the intention of reprimanding him, I found myself facing a man convinced of the right course of his action, someone who expressed only contempt for the exemplary educational concepts that I endeavored to expound to him. By this time, I considered the only method of reasoning with the man was to face him with his own logic.

"Isn't it wrong, Abu Salim," I said, "to beat an orphan?"

The man crossed his arms, thrust his head forward, and bellowed: "Orphan? His father's a blockhead! His shoulders are as big as the world!"

"You mean to say Hamid has a father?" I asked.

Without any variation in tone, the same answer was arrogantly repeated. "His father's a blockhead!"

The insult stung me. It hurt me that the boy should have gained my compassion on the grounds of his lies. I choked on my own gullibility, and all the concessions I'd allowed him in marks now turned round to accuse me of the error of my ways.

All the way home, Abu Salim's words kept resounding inside my head, over and over again. I told myself that these confounded boys were in reality much older than their years, and that my mistake lay in treating them as if they were simply children. I'd ignored the fact of their being so much in advance of their years, and capable of attaining their goal by any means that occurred to them—and that Hamid's duplicity was consonant with the trickery that a cake vendor uses on a half-drunk customer, selling him one cake for the price of two.

No matter how much I tried to convince myself to the contrary, I couldn't shake off an acute feeling of having been grossly insulted by Hamid, and my thoughts inclined towards revenge. In retrospect I can now view the issue as trivial, and my thinking even more so, but at the time I was obsessed by the desire to avenge myself for the insult.

What happened subsequently did nothing to abate my rage; on the contrary, it served only to whip up the already tempestuous flames. The situation was worsened when a talkative student related to me how Hamid's mother had died a few months before, after giving birth to a dead baby girl. I found myself plunged into the web of lies Hamid had spun around me with consummate skill.

My patience finally came to an end one hot afternoon. I was on my way back from school when I suddenly saw him after a long absence. It seemed uncanny that I should meet him in the same place where I'd first seen him.

He was squatting behind his paint-stained wooden box, staring up at the street, hoping to detain a pair of shoes, while I stood there looking on, dumbfounded, almost unable to believe that I was staring at the alleged cake vendor. I felt the insult return to affront me. When I regained consciousness of what I was doing, I found myself grasping him by the collar, and shaking him relentlessly, while all the time I was shouting: "You liar!"

He looked up at me with dilated eyes that showed sudden hints of fear. His lips moved without articulating a word, while his small effort to get free of my grip failed.

I went on repeating my indictment, although I could feel something capitulating inside, in the face of the despairing silence.

"You liar!" I reiterated.

"Sir?"

He said it slowly, raised a finger mechanically, looked around him fearfully, then confessed in a tremulous voice: "Yes sir, I'm a liar, but listen..."

"I don't want to hear a thing," I said sharply.

He screwed his eyes up and I imagined that he was about to cry.

His voice was still shaking when he said: "Listen, sir."

"You liar," I cut him short. "You live with your mother, isn't that so?"

"No, sir, no! My mother's dead, but it's difficult to explain... When she died, my father asked us to keep her death a secret."

I relaxed my grip, and asked him in a quieter tone: "Why?"

"Because he didn't have the money to pay for the funeral, and he was afraid of the government."

I let my arms fall to my side, sympathizing with the boy's irrational fear, which persisted to this day, but I was still apprehensive that I was being further deceived. I shouted at him again, only this time more gently: "And your father? You told me he was dead...isn't that so?"

Hamid could no longer contain himself. He turned his head to the wall and began crying. I heard his voice, strangled by tears: "My father's not dead, he's mad. He wanders the streets of the city half-naked. He went mad after he saw my brother's head chopped off by the lift."

"Mad?"

"Yes, my brother put his head out of the lift to greet my father, and my father saw the whole thing with his own eyes. It was after that he took to roaming the streets."

My head was beginning to spin.

"Why did you tell me that you sell cakes?" I said. "Are you ashamed of what you do?"

His features relaxed, and he stared at me with lucid eyes.

"No," he said shyly."I used to sell cakes, but the day before yesterday I came back to this job."

"But you used to earn more?" I questioned.

"Yes," he said, "but..."

He hung his head, as was his practice whenever he felt unduly vulnerable, and with his brush proceeded to beat the top of his box. Without raising his eyes, he whispered: "When I got hungry at the end of the night, I'd eat two or three of my cakes."

I didn't know how to react. I endeavored to run off, but found myself too weak to do so. The small head with the wiry black hair remained bent. Without knowing why, I raised my foot and placed it firmly on the hump of the box.

The skillful hands set to work, while the rough head nodded rhythmically over the shoe, and then that same voice reached me, saying simply: "Sir...you haven't changed your shoes in a year. These shoes are cheap."

The Cat

While he was waiting in the café, it suddenly occurred to him to go to Samira's. He apologized to his card partners, pushed back his chair and went out into the street. The heat inflamed his head, but nothing could weaken his resolve to see her, so he hailed the first taxi he encountered, jumped into the back seat, and instructed the driver on how to reach his destination.

When he had settled down in his seat, he began to question his motives for visiting Samira. A voice in his head suggested the possibility that he was deceiving himself. "You're a liar, you're just going to see her because you've nowhere else to go. Fear of a vacuum is what's driving you towards her."

He smiled proudly to himself, arrogantly dismissing the idea. "I'm going to her because I want to be with her," he assured himself.

As the car accelerated down the road, he felt a small lump in his throat, a symptom which occurred whenever he anticipated excitement. He noticed too that the veins on the back of his hand were protruding. He began whistling to distract himself, and reassured himself again that the reason for his going to visit Samira was that he really wanted to see her. It wasn't his first visit after all.

He stared out of the window at the people in the street; they were like a chain of ants, each one following his particular path, no one knowing whence he came or where he was going. And he reflected that he was a person who lived fully, doing what he wanted; going where he wanted. His life to date had passed without any major crisis, and he was convinced that with his special powers it would continue to do so. What could interrupt the even tenure of his days? He could vividly recall how he visited Samira on the day his father died. He had once confided to a friend that in this world, Samira was everything to him. She was the only thing whose beginning and end he knew. When would these ant-like people understand that Samira was the truth, that everything else was just a wrapper around a wrapper, and that there was no truth but her? He realized, suddenly, that he was superior to all the ant-like people. And yet, he reflected, what was it that made him superior?

He shook his head, unable to discover the reason; it wasn't something immediately locatable, it was rather an instinctive conviction, a force exploding inside his body, flooding his veins and throat. That would have to be reason enough for the time being. "Where would you like me to stop, Sir" the taxi driver asked. "Anywhere close to here," he answered.

He examined the aged face of the driver while he paid him, and it occurred to him that the driver knew where he was going; yet he felt no sense of shame, rather he smiled at him and said to himself: 'It's necessary for this driver to exist in order to bring me here, and it's necessary for Samira to exist so that I can receive pleasure.'

These thoughts consolidated his feelings of superiority, for the driver knew, it seemed, that he had brought him where he could find pleasure, and Samira knew that she had to please him. He made his way through a series of narrow alleys that led to Samira's place, feeling himself a small pivot around which all of life revolved.

He felt at ease with the situation, a sense of well-being governed his body, except that the lump in his throat was growing larger. 'Good' he thought, 'that shows that I still love her.'

Formerly, no sooner had he knocked at Samira's door than his desire for her had abated, and he had felt the lump dissolve in his throat, so that the act had taken place without any desire. This invariably left him with a feeling of frustration; but today everything seemed primed for success.

'If only Samira lived in a house on a main street,' he reflected, 'then she'd save me the ignominy of walking through this miserable alley. Why doesn't she live somewhere where it's convenient to drive up and park?' The alleyway was still bristling with people, but they grew fewer as he went farther into it.

It seemed incongruous that none of these people knew that he was on his way to visit Samira, and perhaps did not even know of her existence, despite their being neighbors. He suppressed a sardonic smile, and felt the urge to stop every man he passed, shake him by the shoulder, and shout out to him: "That's your bad luck!"

This done, he would continue on his way to her; only why didn't Samira live on a road wide enough to accommodate a car?

'Perhaps she's afraid of the police' he thought, 'or perhaps it's a question of money. It doesn't matter. What really matters is that the room's spacious and comfortable, and that Samira...'

The lump was continuing to grow in his throat, in response to his mood of euphoria, when suddenly he saw a cat.

It was sitting upright in a wet corner of the alley, its tail perfectly straight, and its unusual immobility was emphasized by the manner in which it craned its neck upwards and observed the passers-by with round eyes.

Almost immediately it occurred to him to wonder why the cat didn't move.

He was still pondering the question, when he came up to the creature, and a violent shudder bristled his spine as he noticed the crushed hind legs of the cat, almost flattened on the ground. The fur was matted with blood that had coagulated, and the legs were so distorted that they seemed to have become dissociated from the body. He looked into the cat's eyes, and found in them a mixture of surrender and anticipation.

He continued on his way to Samira's place, and it seemed to him, as he knocked on the door, and afterwards as he kissed Samira as usual and sat down opposite her, that he'd forgotten the entire incident.

It was she who was preoccupying his thoughts. Was it an illusion that from a distance she appeared to be an enchanted mountain magnetizing people to her, and yet in close-up she was no more than just a pile of rocks lacking any real significance. "There must be an explanation for this sort of thing," he told himself. His frenzied attraction to this bewitching creature was founded on something that remained inexplicable to him. Even though he didn't understand why, he still felt the desire to embrace this mountain, in the hope that he would be able to intermingle with it somehow. Lust was kindled in him, and the lump was wounding his throat like a double-edged knife.

"You're very pale," Samira said."Aren't you well?"

The question made him realize that it must have been a speeding car that had smashed the poor cat's legs. But how could a car enter that narrow alley?

"You're ill," Samira repeated. "You've gone paler...would you like some tea?" "Tea" he said. "No! But tell me, could a cat whose hind legs have been smashed crawl from the top of the alley to the water hydrant in the middle?"

"A cat crawl? What's got into you?" Samira asked, puzzled. "Do you have a fever?"

When Samira got up to make some tea, he felt the heat of his sweat-beaded forehead with the back of his hand. 'It must be the sun,' he told himself. 'I don't have a fever.' He relaxed in the comfortable chair and tried to forget himself for a little while.

'A whore's room has a special smell,' he found himself thinking. 'No doubt it springs from a particular spot... the bed? The curtains? Or from my own nose? It's a peculiar, distinct smell. I can sniff it out like a trained dog... A dog? What was it that had brought the cat to the middle of the alley?' He adjusted his position. Samira returned in her rosy nightgown carrying the tea. He stared at her body and felt that his desire had decreased.

Then she said: "I've been thinking about what you asked. Was the cat almost dead?"

He thought for a little while, and said, "Yes, I think so. It appeared to be waiting..."

"Then it probably crawled into the alley to die there," Samira said.

"But why in that particular place?" he asked.

"Ask it," she said. "I'm not a cat!"

She laughed with an abandon that was appropriate to her, then she came and sat by his side and placed her soft arm around his shoulders, while he kept asking himself what power it was that induced the animal to crawl from the road into the middle of the alley?

He suddenly jumped free of her embrace, violently shaking his head, and began to pace around the room, distractedly, desperately seeking a less depressing topic to engage his attention.

"Why do you live here?" he said. "Why don't you find yourself a house in a street that would save your customers the trouble of walking down this miserable alley?"

Samira laughed...she got up and lay down on the bed with affected tiredness, then said, looking at him out of the corners of her eyes:

"I live here so that only customers who really desire me make the effort to come. The uncertain ones don't bother to make it to the end of the alley. They go somewhere else. Others, like you, burn to get here."

He put his hands in his pockets and began pacing the room again. His head spun with a whirlpool of colorless nausea, as he remembered her words: "Others, like you, burn to get here." He stared blankly at the wall so as to shut out the sentence that had begun to howl like a lost wolf in his head. At eye level there was a picture of a foaming waterfall. Directly beneath it was a cheap marble statue of a naked woman without a head, then a table, a chair behind it, a mirror, and the bed on which she reclined smoking.

He heard her voice, seductive with femininity, its tone aimed at arousing him.

"As for those who really want me, the way you do, they walk here."

"So that's how it was?" he said abruptly.

"What?" she said, startled.

"He crawled here...the cat...dragging his crushed legs behind him, dragged himself here to die?"

Samira shifted her position, and shouted to him in a hurt voice: "What on earth's gotten into you today? You're mad...I've never known you to act like this before. Do you think I'm a teacher to be asked questions all the time?"

Her voice still resounded as he put his money on the table and went out into the miserable alley.

Pearls in the Street

The radio fell silent, and I could hear a worn out clock striking from the far end of the city. Then, suddenly, the sound of the radio came back and a wanton song blared out, interrupted by a voice celebrating the coming of the new year.

But the room and the people in it remained as silent as before, in a way that was difficult to explain. Were we silent, I wondered, because we'd taken leave of a year heavy with suffering, or because we were entering another year apparently no less full of suffering, or for the two reasons together?

Someone had to clear the suffocating atmosphere, and it was Hasan who suggested we go out onto the balcony and breathe in the new year air before the others breathed it and cheapened it for us. It was pitch black and there was a red glow right out on the horizon where the oil companies were burning their unwanted gas. The flames danced in a futile attempt to light up the whole sky, and every now and then, they'd fall, bathing the ground in light, before flaring up again.

"We earn a lot," said Hasan, leaning against the railings of the balcony while the rest of us sat down on the low window ledges. "We really earn a lot. And yet there are people who never get to smell a well-cooked meal."

We were fed up with moral lessons like this. We knew all about people who wasted away looking for a means of livelihood, and we also knew, in minute detail, about the heroism of those who came from afar to find a living and died from the weary effort of striving for it. We didn't need a new lesson in morals from this dreamer devouring the horizon with his glowering eyes and leaning on the ledge of the balcony like a poet.

But Hasan's voice reached us again, with a note of defiance in it now.

"I could tell you about something that happened exactly a year ago, right at the beginning of last year. I was involved in it."

He fell silent again, apparently not wanting to say any more. Then he went on.

"A person ought to die at the beginning of the year or the end of it. That way people will remember the date of his death better than if he'd died on an ordinary day. My friend, who's the hero of this story, died at the start of the year. That's why it's difficult for us to forget his death and why we can't forget his story either."

Reluctantly one of us had to ask.

"What story's that?"

"A really strange story, sir. I've tried not to think about it all through this year; I was afraid people would think I was lying or that I'd find it unbelievable myself. But now, at the beginning of a new year, I can't put it out of my mind—why I've no idea, but I can't. I've got to tell you about it. It may do me good to get it off my chest."

Hasan turned, and we saw a face clouded by a tragedy as gloomy as his features. Out on the horizon the red flames flared right up, then died back down to the ground.

"I hadn't realized," Hasan said, "that Saad would follow me here. We grew up together as children, it's true, but later on I got diplomas where he didn't, so I had a better chance of making a living than he did. And yet he came here, fired with an ambition to make something of himself, and he never lost his enthusiasm.

"I made him welcome in my house and looked after him as well as I could, but I wasn't able to do anything to help him find a job. He was completely unequipped for the struggle to get into a government department—without a diploma all he got was a hand stretched out ready to give him a brutal slap in the face! I was prepared to bear with Saad al-Din for as long as necessary, but every now and then I felt obliged to point out to him that there was no real prospect of a job and that he ought to go back to his home town, where he'd be able to solve his problems in one way or another. I told him the wheel that revolved here was legendary for its harshness and didn't give a damn for individual human beings. Hunger, I told him, was merely an amusing spectacle for people living in luxury; people here were straining after every penny and didn't turn back to look at the others crawling behind them. But Saad al-Din wasn't bothered in the least. He told me once that he couldn't go back with no job and no money; he'd never be able to face anyone, friend or foe, as they asked him (if they didn't simply whisper or point, or say nothing to him at all) how he could possibly return from the valley of gold with no gold.

"O Saad al-Din!

"Every now and then I'd tell him: 'Look, Saad al-Din, the money you brought with you won't last much longer, and then what are you going to do? Do you expect your friends to keep you in their homes forever? Your health won't let you live any old how; you've a serious heart problem which needs total rest and a good diet. What you want in your condition is a family life, not a casual bachelor existence! If you've got the return fare in your pocket, you should go back.'

"But Saad al-Din wouldn't listen. He wanted to stay on in the bustling city where things never stopped—searching, going around, wandering, looking for something.

"To cut a long short, my friends, he came to me one day to say that the little money that he'd had was almost gone. He was trapped, he said: he couldn't go on much longer, and he couldn't go back. What could he do? All I could do was offer to pay his fare home, but he refused this. Like everyone else who comes here, he wanted a miracle, a miracle to fill his pockets with gold, and take him very gently by the hand and lead him home on a red carpet! God knows I did my best to talk him out of it, and fearing that he might still hesitate, I persuaded him to go straight to the nearest travel agent with me, so that we could fix a date for him to leave soon.

"It was a cold, overcast day, I remember. As we walked through the streets together, Saad al-Din's silence made me feel unbearably embarrassed, and I decided to remain silent too. Presently his agitated voice broke out, and I felt his hand tugging violently at my sleeve. I turned towards him to see his eyes glittering with the desperation of a last appeal.

"'Listen, Hasan,' he said, almost entreating, 'I believe that somewhere in the infinite blue there's some kind of God, and I don't believe for a moment that he'll abandon me. There's a new path open to me, and I must take it.'

"'What sort of path?' I enquired.

"'Look over there,' he said. 'Do you see that man sitting in front of a basket in the middle of the square? Do you know what he sells?'

"I looked across the square and saw a wretched looking man squatting in front of a small basket. He had no customers, and it was cold too.

"'I don't know,' I replied.

"'He sells oysters,' said Saad al-Din. 'His basket's full of the shells he collects and he sells them at four for a rupee. Only God knows whether the shell has a pearl in it or not. This is the most exciting lottery anyone could find in a lifetime.'

"'You're not going to try it?' I asked.

"'I must try my luck.'

"'What luck?'

"'The luck that's buried under the rubble of ten years of solid suffering. If I put the money I've got left into buying shells, I'm bound to find a pearl.'

"It seemed as though Saad al-Din had lost his better judgement. All the years of suffering, the mental torment, the hopeless attempts to survive had, together, led him to this: the belief that success lay in a trick, in the haphazard chance of discovering the rare in the commonplace. He'd convinced himself that the riches and comfort he aspired to resided in the shell of a randomly picked oyster.

"But to tell you the truth, the prospect of finding a pearl made me feel thoroughly excited too. Perhaps it would turn out to be a big round pearl, tinged with blue from the current of an unknown ocean. It didn't appear altogether impossible that Saad al-Din would find a pearl, and so be able to carry on with his life here or return home with some vestige of riches.

"We moved towards the man squatting in front of his fishy basket. I was still afraid, in spite of everything, that Saad al-Din would find failure again. I made one last attempt to reason with him.

"'I suppose you know,' I said, 'that you've got one chance in a thousand? Do you know that there's only one pearl found in every thousand oyster shells, and that precious cargo may be no larger than a lentil grain?'

"'Hasan,' he answered, 'just consider, there are millions of shells on the seabed. How can you be sure that the diver didn't pick up the pregnant one and leave the empty one?' And with that, Saad al-Din proceeded to exchange all the money in his pocket for a small pile of shells from the heap. As I watched the transaction, I was once again convinced of the imprudence of his scheme.

"The man's knife grated on the shells. Each time, with the skill of a craftsman, he slid his knife into the top of the shell where the sun had made an opening large enough to fit the tip of the blade. Then he worked the knife in a circular movement and prized open the shell to reveal the mollusc inside—a sticky mass like tender meat or the entrails of a young animal. The knife point probed the flesh, which was discarded in a bin. Disappointment registered on his face, then lessened at the prospect of new hope, as the knife once again performed its circular incision.

"The pile of shells was decreasing, and an aura that was supernatural invested the situation with mystery. Saad al-Din's eyes hung on the curve of the blade, as, with the utmost simplicity, he performed his familiar task. As I watched him, I could see the ordeal was sucking away at his fortitude with a thousand clinging tentacles.

"Finally, the ordinary developed into the bizarre. There was only one shell left. Exhaustion was written on Saad al-Din's face, and I observed him with alarm as his fingers unlocked the darkness of the shell. Saad al-Din looked terrible. He had the face of a man hanging over an abyss and about to tumble in. So intense was his desire to see a pearl appear in the last shell.

"A terrifying glitter flashed, suddenly, in his anxious eyes, and it seemed to me that the whole of life was contained in that one transmission of light. He was staring at the shell and I was looking at his face. Then, before I knew what was happening, Saad al-Din fell on his face in the mud. When I tried to pick him up, I found that he was dead."

*　*　*　*　*

It was still pitch black outside. The red flames leapt forcefully on the horizon, and as suddenly died away. The silence grew deeper; none of us felt like talking. It didn't matter at that moment whether Hasan had imagined the events he described, or exaggerated them or lied about them; we were still spellbound by the story. When Hasan spoke again, his voice betrayed the tension and the strain.

"The poor man had a weak heart," he said. "The situation was too much for him, and I still can't decide whether he died from the elation of seeing a pearl in that last shell, or from disappointment because he knew it was empty. Everything happened so quickly I had no time to think. The sight of his body lying there in the mud made me forget all about shells and pearls, and of course, by the time we'd taken away the body the man with the shells had disappeared."

A Concise Principle

Abd al-Jabbar was a philosopher, and since childhood he had come to evaluate life in terms of a theory. He formulated a question for himself which was to preoccupy him for an entire week, so profound was the manner of his reflection. The conundrum was this: why do people wear hats on their heads and shoes on their feet? Another time he speculated on why people didn't walk on all fours like animals, a mode of transport surely more conducive to comfort?

As time progressed, so the quality of his reflections improved, until he was able to compound a concise principle: 'As man was born without prior consultation, why shouldn't he have the freedom to choose the method of his end?' And from this premise, he proceeded to the more concise principle that 'death is the summation of life.'

His way of thought brought with it a tranquility that he prized above all things, and he anticipated that time in which he would commence choosing the intended manner of his death.

It follows that those who claim that Abd al-Jabbar joined the revolution against his will lack the knowledge that he chose of his own volition to go to the volunteer center, stand before the officer, who had not as yet found an appropriate military uniform, and say in a steady voice: "I want a rifle to participate in the revolution."

He soon learned that, if he wished to join the revolution, he would have to find a rifle in one way or another, and that this would not be easy.

"I might die before I get a rifle," he said to the officer angrily. He fell silent, however, at the officer's answer, which was unexpected, yet contained an element of truth: "Have you just come here to enjoy the summer and then go home?"

In the light of this supposition, Abd al-Jabbar considered that his philosophy needed modifying slightly, as he would probably die before acquiring a rifle. Thus he arrived at a new concise principle. 'The important thing,' he thought, 'is not that a man dies and is subsequently ennobled, but that he should find himself a noble idea before he dies!'

But it so happened that Abd al-Jabbar managed to gain possession of an almost new rifle without expanding the effort he'd imagined was needed for its acquisition, and also without applying his philosophic precepts to the dilemma. He had gone outside in the aftermath of a morning battle, and found a dead soldier. The dead don't need rifles, he'd reasoned, as he turned over the dead body, and uncovered a French rifle with a pointed muzzle.

To his comrades on the barricade Abd al-Jabbar was known as "the philosopher." The soldiers found in his philosophy a meaning suitable to justify the events that took place. Most of the revolutionaries were youths, and it pleased him to realize that he was their senior, and that his authority was sufficient to assemble them after each battle, so that they might assimilate his new concise principle concerning death; a philosophy that changed in accordance with the casualties.

One dark night, an illiterate peasant died, and before falling on the barricade cursed a certain leader and his men. In thinking of a suitable elegy in which to mourn the martyr's death, Abd al-Jabbar formulated his new concise principle: 'The noble idea does not require thought, it demands feeling.' On the following night, a young man who'd emerged from the barricades, knife in hand, to attack a soldier crawling near the wall, was shot on his way back to the shelter. As a consequence, Abd al-Jabbar thought: 'Courage is the measure of loyalty.'

Abd al-Jabbar was notable for his courage, and as a result of this virtue the officer, who had at last acquired a suitable military uniform, asked him to make a reconnaissance of the harbor. He believed that the philosopher's sad, calm face would arouse no suspicion in the hearts of the enemy.

Abd al-Jabbar walked the streets unarmed. He reached the harbor and wandered around at will, before turning back in

the direction of his barricade. But contrary to expectation, someone who'd once taken part in an attack recognized him, and he
was first apprehended, then taken to a frightened officer, who,
after slapping him, said:

"You're a revolutionary?"

"Yes," Abd al-Jabbar replied.

"You swine!"

"No!" he exclaimed to the officer.

While he was being remorselessly beaten, Abd al-Jabbar
did not omit to formulate a new concise principle: 'The beating
of a prisoner is an arrogant expression of fear.' And having
pondered this, he felt some comfort.

While Abd al-Jabbar engaged in reflection, the officer,
prompted by his closest supporters, arrived at what he considered to be an astute conclusion to the situation; one which their
captive considered to be yet another arrogant form of behavior
arising from fear.

The officer addressed him: "You will proceed in front of
us to your cursed barricade, and declare to your crazy comrades
that you've brought a fresh party of revolutionaries with you.
That done, my soldiers will finish things off."

"And what about me?" enquired Abd al-Jabbar.

"You'll either be honored with your life," replied the officer, "or, in the event of your betraying us, you'll die like a
dog." Abd al-Jabbar silently said to himself: 'Betrayal is a despicable form of death.'

Head high, Abd al-Jabbar walked in front of two
columns of soldiers, the muzzle of an automatic rifle digging
into his waist. Just before they arrived at the barricades, he
heard the rasping voice of the officer hiss in the dark: "Now!"

He wasn't afraid, and his comrades said later they de-
tected no tremor in his voice, as he shouted:

"I've brought you fifty soldiers."

He still wasn't dead when his comrades rushed to where
he was lying among the corpses of the soldiers. With great difficulty, one of them heard him utter his final concise principle:

"It's not important if one of us dies. The important thing is to carry on."

Then he died.

Eight Minutes

Ali was tired when he left work, and although it was his custom to walk the distance home, he decided, for once, to hire a taxi. On the journey there, he found himself preoccupied with the unresolved issue of the day. What continued to bother him was the question of his vacation. When should he take it, and how should he spend it, and where was he to go? Each year the same problem arose, and presented the same difficulties. When the cab arrived at his building, he gave the fare to the driver, nodded with evident pride to the janitor and walked towards the lift.

There, while waiting for what he called "the coffin" to descend, he was faced with the unwelcome knowledge that he'd forgotten the keys to his apartment. Almost at once he remembered that he'd left them on his desk in the office. He debated what to do, and turned round on his heels.

"What's wrong, Sayyid Ali?"

"Nothing, nothing at all, Taysir," he replied. "I've simply forgotten my keys."

"I can open the door from inside," Taysir said, "but can you remember whether you left your balcony doors open?"

"The balcony doors?" he asked. "You mean you propose to jump from the adjacent balcony to mine?"

"Yes," the janitor answered calmly, his voice dispelling any fear that such a proposal would arouse in Sayyid Ali's mind. For a person to jump from one balcony to the next, on the ninth floor, was no small matter, for the wall that divided the two balconies jutted out from the building; going around it at that incredible height would be sure to induce vertigo. The deep calm in Taysir's voice compelled Sayyid Ali to say: "Yes, Taysir, I'm quite sure I left the balcony doors open."

* * * * *

When the lift arrived, Taysir opened the door, then let it close behind him. The old watch on his wrist pointed to seven minutes past two; the red hand was revolving round its axis like a little devil... Taysir let his arm fall negligently to his thigh, and proceeded to scrutinize his face in the broken mirror of the lift. There was a taste of cottonseed in his mouth, and his breathing was somewhat labored. 'No, I'm not afraid,' he told himself. He nodded his head at the mirror and smiled, exaggerating the O of his mouth, stretched out his arms to lean against the lift walls, and, bending slightly towards his reflection, stared at the blue circles drawn around his eyes.

In his head was an idea encased in a cocoon of violet silk, around which a wasp made dilatory circles. Still the idea was there, and the wasp was refusing to penetrate the inner chamber of his mind. Soon he would get to apartment No.13, which had never had an occupant even for half a day. On his way to the balcony he'd pass the bathroom door, inside which he was sure to see a cockroach turned on its back, simulating death, and on arriving at the bedroom he would, he knew, encounter small balls of dust wrapped around strands of hair. How does hair contrive to get into a room which has never been occupied? Then he'd turn the knob on the glass door of the balcony... No, it was better not to think about it; he knew that he was afraid. He folded his arms across his chest and distracted himself by thinking of small things like how the lift would have to be repaired one day—its slow crawl resembled that of a snake without a tail. This, he knew, was simply to distance himself from the violet cocoon, for fear of its magnetic attraction. He tried instead to think of something frivolous. What if the lift were to go on ascending until it reached the roof, and then still went on, without stopping? 'Taysir,' he said to himself, 'you're terrified.' He stared at the mirror again, widening his smile, overcome by a boyish impulse to put out his tongue; but the lift came to a halt, and his heart started throbbing. He convinced himself that this was because the lift had come to an abrupt stop, something that always triggered off this spontaneous reaction.

Then he contemplated his strategy. He would first place his hand on the wall separating the two balconies, then lift one leg in order to place a foot on the edge of the blue iron barrier, after which he would place his palm on the other side of the dividing wall. Having come so far, it would be necessary at this point to place his other leg at the foot of the barrier, so as to achieve balance. He was deep in reverie when he pushed open the lift door and began searching in his pockets for the keys to the untenanted apartment. It was with a feeling of disappointment that he saw the first key fit apartment 13.

On the way to the balcony he tried not to think. His head was full of transient blue dust. He hummed a brief song, then lapsed into silence. By the time he closed his hand around the knob of the balcony door, the colored wasp had closed in on the violet cocoon, and was hovering directly above it. 'People never rent this flat' he told himself, 'because it carries an ill-omened number; the apartment's unlucky...' He felt an overwhelming impulse to let go of the door knob and retrace his footsteps to the lift; but the decision binding him was irrevocable. He shook his head repeatedly, opened the door and took rapid strides to the blue barrier of the balcony.

'I'm on the ninth floor,' he told himself, looking down to be sure that nothing had changed.

He could see Sayyid Ali standing on the pavement with one hand in his pocket and the other holding a newspaper with which he slapped his thigh. A small car was parked nearby; it looked like a squashed dog.

Taysir was conscious of the violet cocoon in his head, with the wasp buzzing over it, still frustrated in its design to discover the secret within. Colorful, sustaining its flight, the wasp appeared to be enjoying the wait. Taysir felt at ease contemplating both, glad of their separation. He leaned over the barrier, but was unable to see whether the door to the other flat was open. He leaned back, took off his jacket and shoes, and once again looked down at the road. 'Even if you're not afraid, Taysir,' he said, 'why are you taking all these risks?'

He answered himself by thinking: 'Sayyid Ali's a good man...I must serve him.' He folded his jacket, placed it next to his shoes on the far side of the balcony, then he returned, and shook the barrier railings with considerable force, to be sure that they were firm. There were no handholds above to assist him, and he found himself thinking: 'Once I bought him some fruit, a few oranges and bananas, and he gave me five liras and smiled.' Still thinking of this, he lifted his foot, placed it on the barrier and put his hand on the wall. The car beneath was still miniaturized to a squashed dog, and he could see Sayyid Ali looking up in his direction. 'So this is what it amounts to,' Taysir commented, 'you go to these lengths to open the door for him, and he'll reward you with ten liras, or perhaps five. Is this really what it's all about? Six liras is the price of the brass engraved earrings that I've been promising my sister for year after year. What if he only gives me five liras, or worse still, nothing at all?'

He transferred his hand to the other wall. Then came the moment of danger, when he lifted his other foot off the ground, and, for an instant, it hung there suspended in the air, while his body adopted the movements of a scorpion balancing on the edge of an object. He pressed his chest against the rough wall, and with the outstretched fingers of his free hand tentatively felt for the far side of the partition, his mind anticipating the next dangerous maneuver in which he'd transfer his leg to it. He felt like a crucified spider, waiting for the moment to be freed from impalement. He shifted a leg; then came two hard moments, during which he was overcome by the desire to look down. He could see the midget-sized Sayyid Ali, and simultaneously felt the irascible wasp reach the cocoon, and violently tear it apart. 'What if your foot should slip, Taysir,' he thought.

* * * * *

108

, By the time Taysir closed the lift door, Sayyid Ali had turned around and walked out into the street. 'Taysir's a courageous lad,' he repeated to himself. 'He takes things like that in his stride.' He was too tired to recognize the dangers involved in such an undertaking, so he looked up, and counted the floors until his eyes found the ninth. It didn't register with him that this was his balcony until he saw the green towel hanging on the line. Taysir hadn't arrived yet, and he remembered that the lift in this building was interminably slow. He went back to reflecting on how things happen without prior intention. Once he'd been waiting for the lift when he felt that someone was standing behind him; he'd turned round, and there was his neighbor, also waiting for the lift. This was the first time they'd met. When the lift arrived, he opened the door for her and then followed inside. 'I must say something' he'd urged himself. 'I must establish some kind of relationship.' The advent of a red light indicated that the lift had arrived at the third floor—a signal that he should find appropriate words in order to make contact. So he said: "This is the slowest lift I've ever been in."

She looked at him with the beginning of a smile, nodded her head, and said: "It certainly is!"

"Do you know," he'd continued, "I used to think it was my presence that made the lift crawl...but now..."

They'd smiled at each other in order to break the tension, and when the lift came to a halt, he'd opened the door, nodded his head meaningfully, and before he could walk out of the lift, had heard her quiet voice say: "I hope you don't take this talk about heavy presence too seriously."

Later that day he'd telephoned her, pretending that he'd been trying to call another apartment, and the ensuing conversation had further encouraged his cause. That noon he'd summoned Taysir, asked him to go out and purchase oranges and bananas, and given him five liras in the hope that he'd say nothing if he happened to notice something going on between him and his neighbor.

He looked up again and searched for the green towel. Taysir still hadn't arrived. When he raised his eyes to the tenth floor, he could see her standing there. She was wearing a white blouse, and leaning with her elbows on the blue iron railings, with her head resting on her palms. He knew that she was looking at him.

He saluted her, and she returned his greeting and straightened up. She was a magnificent woman, who had put things in their true perspective from the very first. Without equivocation she'd said to him: "All that I want from you is the same as what you want from me, so don't let's complicate the issue."

Taysir was visible now. He peered over the blue railings, took off his jacket and bent down to remove his shoes. At the same time, his neighbor signalled to him from the tenth floor, anxious to know what was going on. He undertook to explain the situation to her in a series of lucid gestures, so that there could be no doubt in her mind as to why Taysir was positioned on the ninth floor.

'What if Taysir should fall?' Sayyid Ali asked himself, as quickly dismissing the notion on the grounds of the young man's courage, and the likelihood that he'd undertaken such a venture before.

If he did fall, Sayyid Ali reflected, then the complications would spoil his intended vacation. Once again he felt disquieted, and thought: 'I must be a despicable person to attach more importance to my vacation than a man's death.' Nevertheless his holiday was important; the idea of it was concealed in his innermost mind, and the thought of its presence there filled him with indescribable joy.

Taysir was on the point of crossing the barrier. Sayyid Ali watched him balance carefully, one hand in the air, the other pressed on the wall, as he slowly and cautiously turned his body around, an action that would complete itself by the forward placement of his right leg. At the same time Taysir turned his head, and for a brief moment Sayyid Ali imagined that he was looking at him. He was about to raise his hand in greeting, when a small scrap of white paper came fluttering through the air towards him, its spiral flight resembling that of a jubilant bird's. He saw his neighbor pointing at the paper in a way that made him understand that it was a message for him.

Sayyid Ali read the note, then walked towards the lift. Simultaneously, Taysir turned himself round, and with one daring leap, negotiating the distance between the two balconies, he landed safely on Sayyid Ali's balcony. He stood there for a while, panting with relief. Beads of perspiration filmed the corners of his mouth, and his palms were also damp with sweat. He took a deep breath. There was a small pain, no larger than a pinprick, in his toes. As he pushed the balcony door open, his head felt hollow; the tension in his chest made him want to cry out. For a split second he imagined that he'd just come back from the sea after a day spent swimming...

He placed his hand on the door-handle, pulled it, and found Sayyid Ali standing in front of him.

"I congratulate you, Taysir," he said. "It was a splendid feat."

Taysir attempted to say something in reply, but the taste of cottonseed oil still permeated his mouth, so he simply shook his head and smiled.

"Taysir, here are twenty-five liras. I want you to buy me a half bottle of whisky and some fruit. You can keep the change."

Taysir smiled, making a quick mental calculation of how much change the purchases would leave him; he reckoned on having about ten liras left. Then he felt a surge of disgust, felt like turning his back and leaving with all possible speed.

"Don't look so gloomy," Sayyid Ali said. "And when you come back with the whisky and fruit, take them straight to the tenth floor."

He winked cheerfully, still standing at the door, and Taysir was left blankly contemplating the twenty-five lira note between his fingers. As an act of unconscious distraction he glanced at his watch. It was exactly 2:15. He looked up again and saw Sayyid Ali smiling at him in recognition, before he slammed the door to his flat. It made a dry, loud bang as it closed behind him. He winked at Taysir again, screwed up the piece of paper between his fingers, and taking the stairs two at a time, let it fall to the ground,

It rolled between Taysir's feet, as his head reverberated with the slamming of Sayyid Ali's door.

Death of Bed 12

My Dear Ahmad,

I've chosen you of all people to be the recipient of this letter for reasons that may appear trivial to you, but which have become, since yesterday, the central preoccupation of my thoughts. I've also chosen to confide in you, because when I saw him yesterday evening, dying on a raised white bed, I recalled how often you used the idea of death to express extremes. Phrases of yours came back to me: "He almost died laughing," or "I'm dead tired," and "Death can't extinguish my love" and so on. It's true that we all use these expressions, but with you they're a way of life. And so I thought of you as I watched him shrink in his bed, tighten his long, thin fingers on the bed cover, go into a convulsion, and then stare at me with dead eyes.

I suppose I should start at the beginning. You doubtless know that I've been in the hospital for the past two months, suffering from an intestinal ulcer. But that's not the important thing, for every time the surgeon patches up my stomach, I have to conceal the "ulcer" in my head about which he knows nothing. And believe me the latter is a much more painful thing. The door of my room opens onto the main corridor of the wing for internal diseases, while the window overlooks the small hospital garden. And so it is that while leaning on my pillow, I'm able to observe both the patients who ceaselessly swarm past my door and the birds who, also ceaselessly, fly past my window. I'm surrounded by people who come here to die under the reassuring scalpel, and whom I see arriving upright on their feet, and departing, after a few days or hours, laid out on the death trolley, wrapped in a white shroud. In the face of this, I find myself impotent to forestall the holes that have begun to open up in my head, and helpless to stop the flow of questions that relentlessly beleaguer me.

I expect to be discharged in a few days, for they've patched up my intestines as best they can. I can now walk supported by the arm of a plain old nurse, and I'm driven to do so by curiosity and instinctive motivation. The treatment's done nothing except to transfer the ulcer from my intestines to my head. Medicine here, as I told my plain old nurse, is limited strictly to physical ailments, and has never advanced sufficiently to find answers to one's mind. The crone laughed at what I said, revealing her black, gapped teeth, and led me calmly to the scales.

But enough of this talk. What really concerns me is the theme of death. And a death that one's witnessed, rather than learned of secondhand. The difference between the two is so vast that only those who've experienced the sight of someone clutching at the bed cover, holding on with all his strength to resist the terrible slide to extinction, can appreciate the difference. It's as if the bed cover could serve as an anchorage from the all-powerful one who, bit by bit, erases this life about which we know so little.

The doctors had grouped around him, and as he lay in his convulsions I was able to read the card hanging at the bottom of his bed. I'd managed to slip away from my room unnoticed, and the doctors were too preoccupied with their dying patient to notice me standing there. The card read: "Name: Muhammad Ali Akbar. Age: 25 years. Nationality: Omani." I turned the card over and read the diagnosis: "Leukemia."

Again I stared at the lean, dark face, the wide, terrified eyes, the lip fibers trembling like purple waves. In the course of their wandering, his eyes had come to rest on my face and I imagined that he was appealing for my help. I tried to think why. Was it because I used to greet him every morning, or because he read in my face a comprehension of the terror he was undergoing? He continued to stare at me, and then quite simply died.

It was only then that I was discovered, and a furious doctor dragged me back to my room, but couldn't distance me from the scene imprinted in my mind's eye. I climbed into bed and heard the nurse's voice in the corridor outside the door, saying matter of factly: "The occupant of Bed 12 has died."

Hearing this, I said to myself: Muhammad Ali Akbar's lost his name; he's Bed 12 now. Yet what do I mean when I personalize him and continue to use his name? Is it of any importance to him now if his name's substituted by a number? Following that train of thought, I recalled how he refused to have any part of his name omitted when addressed. Each morning the nurse would ask him: "How are you today, Muhammad Ali?" and he'd refuse to answer, for he considered his name to be Muhammad Ali Akbar, pronounced like that, all in one go, and that this abbreviation adopted by the nurse belonged to some other person.

The nurses found plenty of cause for humor in this insistence on the indivisibility of his name, but Muhammad Ali Akbar never once made concessions on this serious point. Perhaps he considered that in laying claims to his rightful name, he was realizing a possession, for he was poor, poorer than you can imagine, idling his time away in cafés. Poverty was pronounced in his face, his hands, his body, in the way he ate, and in the objects that surrounded him.

When I was able for the first time after the operation to walk by myself, I visited him. The top part of his bed was raised and he was sitting in a state of reverie. I sat on the edge of the bed for a short time and engaged in a brief and desultory talk with him. My attention was drawn to an old wooden box, firmly tied with a piece of hemprope, that he kept next to his pillow, and on which his name was carved in a form of Persian calligraphy. With the exception of this, he owned nothing in the world apart from his few clothes hanging in the hospital wardrobe. I remember asking the nurse: "What's in that old box?"

"No one knows," she replied, laughing. "He refuses to part with it even for a minute." Then she leaned over and whispered: "These people who look poor are very often hiding a fortune. The box might have all his wealth in it."

No one visited him during his stay in the hospital. As he knew no one, I used to send him some of the sweets and cakes that my visitors so generously brought me. He received them without enthusiasm, and his complete lack of gratitude evoked a degree of passing resentment in me.

I wasn't interested in the mystery of his box, and despite his constantly deteriorating condition, his relation to it didn't change. In view of this, the nurse's opinion was that if the box had contained some kind of fortune, he would surely have distributed it by now or made provision by creating a legacy. I laughed as the young do at the apparent stupidity of her remarks; how could she expect Muhammad Ali Akbar to calmly accept and rationalize his imminent death? It was rather that the box had come to represent a symbol of permanence, and by subscribing to its durability he was insisting on the possibility of his own survival.

When Muhammad Ali Akbar finally died, with the box dutifully next to him, I considered it our responsibility to see that the unopened box was buried with him. I lodged the thought in my mind and returned to my room; but throughout that night I didn't sleep. Although Muhammad Ali Akbar had been taken to the autopsy room wrapped in a white sheet, he appeared to be sitting in my room, staring at me, or else walking the corridors of the hospital, checking his bed, and once I thought I could hear him gasp as he breathed out before falling asleep. By the time day broke over the trees in the hospital garden, I'd formed a complete story about him, for myself.

* * * * *

Muhammad Ali Akbar was a poor man from the western neighborhood of the village of Ibkha in Oman. A lean, brown youth, his eyes had burned with the potential of unrealized ambition. He was poor and had never known a life other than one of poverty. Everyone in Ibkha accepted their lot, and enjoyed the simplicity of life without giving thought to the acquisition of material gain. So it was that the two waterskins that Muhammad Ali Akbar carried on his shoulders, going from door to door to sell water, were the balancing scales that gave measure to his life. He was aware of a sense of displacement whenever he let go of his burden, and each morning, when he took up his load again, he would feel that his life was proceeding with tranquility, that he was secured on a balanced path that offered no deviation from his routine habits.

It might have been possible for Muhammad Ali Akbar's life to proceed indefinitely in this organized fashion. And so it would have, had fate been as remote from Oman as civilization. Not even Oman was spared the caprices of fate, and Muhammad Ali Akbar was to prove its unwilling victim.

It happened on a scorchingly hot day. The sandy road was ablaze long before the sun had reached its zenith, and a northerly breeze from the desert dusted his face with sand. He'd knocked at a door and, from behind its crack, a dark young girl with big black eyes had peered out. It all occurred with incredible speed. He'd stood there like someone who'd lost his way, the two waterskins swaying on his slender shoulders, staring at her insensibly, wishing as a person dazed by sunstroke might that his eyes had the magic power to embrace and squeeze her. She'd exchanged looks with him out of sheer amazement; then, finding himself unable to utter a word, he'd turned around and pursued his journey home.

Muhammad Ali Akbar was noted for his shyness, even in the presence of his family, but the incident inspired him sufficiently to confide the whole matter to his eldest sister. His mother had long since died of smallpox and his father was an invalid who was paralyzed. Thus it was he asked for his sister's advice, for he was confident in a way that brooked no discussion that his sister Sabika enjoyed a degree of intelligence and balanced judgement that would enable her to cast light on his problem. She seated herself opposite him on the mat, and, enveloped in her thick black dress, remained silent until Muhammad Ali Akbar had panted out the last of his story.

117

Then she said: "I'll ask for her hand. Isn't that what you want?"

"Yes, yes," he replied. "Do you think there's a chance?"

His sister plucked a straw from the old mat, and replied: "Why not? You're a young man now, and we're all equal in Ibkha."

Muhammad Ali Akbar spent the night burning with anxiety, and when he rose at dawn he found his sister in a corresponding state of nervous anticipation. They agreed to meet at home at noon, so that she could present him with the results of her endeavors, and together decide on a plan to bring the matter to completion.

Muhammad Ali Akbar didn't know how he passed the intervening time, except that he wandered through the alleys with the waterskins on his shoulders. He kept on staring at his shadow, waiting for it to form a circle round his feet so that he could return home. At last it was noon and he retraced his steps back to the house. His sister met him at the door: "Her mother seems agreeable," she said, "but it has to be put to her father. He'll give his answer in five days."

Muhammad Ali Akbar felt assured that he'd succeed in his marriage proposal, and from that day on he began, in his imagination, to conceive of a future with the small, dark beauty. His sister Sabika viewed the situation with a feeling of equanimity. Experience told her that her brother was respected by the community of Ibkha, and her hopes of a successful resolution were confirmed by the importance she attached to a mother's agreement, for she was aware of how a woman can present any idea to her husband and convince him of it as if it were his own. Trusting to her conviction, Sabika felt totally reassured as to the outcome of the matter.

On the fifth day, Sabika went to the girl's house to learn of their decision. When she returned her face was marked with signs of failure. She stood in a corner of the room, unable to meet her brother's eyes and not knowing how to begin. At last she composed herself, and said: "You'll have to forget her, Muhammad Ali."

Unable to summon up words for his bewilderment, he waited for her to finish what she had to say. Sabika took advantage of his silence to continue: "Her father died two days ago, and his last wish to his family was that his daughter shouldn't marry you."

Muhammad Ali heard the words as if they'd been uttered to a stranger, but he still couldn't help asking: "But why, Sabika? Why?"

"He was told that you were a scoundrel who lived by stealing sheep on the mountain road and selling them to foreigners."

"Me?" Muhammad Ali gasped incredulously.

Sabika was unable to maintain the composure of her voice, and she trembled visibly as she said: "They thought you were Muhammad Ali. You know, the one who's a scoundrel. Her father mistook you for him."

He spread his palms out, appealing like a child forced to justify a fault he hadn't committed: "But I'm not Muhammad Ali, I'm Muhammad Ali Akbar."

"It was a mistake," his sister said. "I didn't think to tell them your full name's Muhammad Ali Akbar. I never thought it was necessary to give the complete name."

Muhammad Ali Akbar felt his chest cave in under the force of the blow, but he remained standing in the same spot, staring at his sister without really seeing her at all. Rage was blinding him, but he attempted a last shot: "Did you tell her mother about the mistake? Did you tell her I'm not Muhammad Ali, but Muhammad Ali Akbar?"

"Yes," his sister replied, "but her father's last wish was that she shouldn't marry you."

"But you know who I really am," he appealed. "I'm Muhammad Ali Akbar, the waterseller."

But what use were his protestations now? Everything had, quite simply, come to an end. The issue had been decided on a misunderstanding, and his hopes had correspondingly died.

It wasn't easy to forget the girl. He found himself inexplicably hovering around her house, hoping to catch a brief glimpse of her. But in the end the realization of his failure turned the love he'd harbored into a savage rage, and finally into hatred. It got to the stage that he could no longer pass that road without the fear that he'd be driven to throw stones at the windows of her house.

From that day on he refused to be addressed except by his full name, Muhammad Ali Akbar, and he disdained to answer anyone who chose to abbreviate it, until his refusal became a habit. Even Sabika, his sister, never dared to shorten his name; he stuck unflinchingly to its full form.

But try as he might, he could never again experience happiness, and slowly Ibkha came to represent a graveyard in his eyes. He refused to marry, despite his sister's insistence, and the idea of riches came to obsess him. He wanted to avenge himself on everything, and to marry a woman with whom he could defy his native town, and thus rectify the wrong he'd suffered. But first of all he had to acquire a fortune, and it was in pursuit of this that he decided to embark for Kuwait.

The distance between Ibkha and Ras el-Khaymah was two hours on foot, and from Ras el-Khaymah to Kuwait was a further three days by sea. The fare for the journey on a dilapidated vessel was seventy rupees, but by risking this sum he had the promise of beginning a new life in Kuwait. In a year or two he'd return to Oman and swagger through the alleys of Ibkha wearing a brilliant white *aba* with a golden hem, like the one he'd seen draped across the shoulders of one of the notables of Ras el-Khaymah who'd come to his village to ask for the hand of a girl in marriage, a girl whose beauty had been heard of in his home town.

The voyage was a hazardous one. The vessel had carried its ambitious passengers across the south, and then headed up north from the straits, aiming for the corner of the gulf. They'd been constantly exposed to the dangers of the sea, but as most aboard were inured to the hardships of life, they were only too ready to cooperate with the crew in their efforts to keep the ship afloat in turbulent seas. And when at last they sighted the coast, and the masts of the boats lying moored in the quiet harbor of Kuwait, Muhammad Ali Akbar found himself responding ambivalently to a reality now divorced from the colorful world of his dreams. He searched in his mind for the key that had brought him here, and it struck him that the fantasies he'd nurtured for so long, of avenging himself on Ibkha, seemed removed and implausible. While the dilapidated vessel approached its berth, navigating a course between the ships at anchor, he was startled, for the duration of a few seconds, into a new sense of reality, and it seemed to him that the dreams he'd fabricated of acquiring wealth were simply a solace for his unrequited love and bore no practical bearing on reality.

The packed streets, the size of the buildings, the grey sky, the incandescent heat, the hot northerly wind, the streets jammed with cars, the serious faces...all of these things seemed to impose a barrier between himself and his dream. He wandered around aimlessly, without direction, in that ocean of people, feeling lost and vertiginous in the swim of faces, and believing with the utmost conviction that those faces which did not so much as look at him were declared enemies, that these people, and their sheer numbers, were the walls obstructing the outset of the road to his new future. Things were not as simple as he'd imagined before leaving Ibkha. Nothing appeared to have connectives here or to be sequential. It seemed the roads he walked were without end, that they circled a wall which embraced everything, and when he came upon a road at sunset that led him to the shore, where once again he found the sea, he stood staring at the distant horizon vanishing into the water. Over there was Ibkha, enveloped in a serene haze. At any rate, he assured himself, it was still there. He knew every quarter of it, how every wall bore its own distinct features, and recollecting it thus he realized that, despite everything, it was dear to his heart. The tears that quite suddenly and unashamedly scalded his face made him feel that he was drowning in a vortex of boiling water.

Muhammad Ali Akbar stood there and cried without embarrassment, for the first time since he'd grown up to be a young man, and at the same time he felt an overwhelming compulsion to have the weight of the two waterskins on his shoulders. He was still staring at the horizon as the night slowly descended around him, creating the impression that he was here in a definite place at a definite time, and that the night was no different from the night in Ibkha. People were asleep in their homes, the streets had grown silent, and punctuating it all was the rhythmic surge of the sea beneath moonlight. He felt comforted, wanted to laugh, but, finding himself unable to do so, cried again.

The dawn brought with it a renewed sense of hope, and he went back to roaming the streets. He knew in order to proceed he had first to establish contact with someone from Oman, and that sooner or later he would find this person who would prove to be a stepping stone to his new future.

As it was, Muhammad Ali Akbar took a job as cleaner in a Government office. He was issued with a bicycle to run errands for his department, and it was through cycling that he came to familiarize himself with the layout of streets and buildings. He grew to establish some form of relationship with his new surroundings, but he was unable to free himself from the feeling that he was being followed by his sister's eyes, and that even here he couldn't be free of the image of the girl's latticed window and the scoundrel Muhammad Ali, who, unwittingly, had been the cause of his disaster.

The months hurried by like the rotating spokes of his wheels, and things began to grow easier. He clung to his small savings with the tenacity of one who dreads that on a sudden impulse he might lose them or have them stolen from him. This was how he first got the idea of making a strong-box in which to keep his savings.

His wealth was of a nature that couldn't be priced. Muhammad Ali Akbar had used a part of his earnings to purchase a transparent, white *aba* with a golden hem, and each evening, when he was alone with his box, he'd take out the carefully packed garment, trace his lean, brown fingers gently over the material and spread it out before him as a map of his dreams. On it he'd trace all the streets of his village, and the low wooden latticed windows, behind which young girls peered out at the street. There, in one corner of the cloak, the past lay dormant, unrevivable, and yet its existence was what endowed the *aba* with especial significance. With the same meticulous gentleness, the lean fingers would refold the *aba* and return it to its wooden box. Only after he'd tied the box securely with a strong piece of hemprope could he prepare himself for sleep.

The box also contained a pair of ceramic earrings for his sister Sabika, and a bottle of perfume, gifts he would give her on his return to Ibkha, as well as a white bundle in which his money was concealed. The bundle was tied in a knot, in the hope that his savings would increase, day by day.

As for his illness, it all began one evening when he was returning his bicycle to the storeroom. He felt something burning his extremities and was shocked to discover that he could have become so weak so quickly. At first he didn't attach much significance to it, for shaking fits would afflict him whenever his longing to see Sabika or return to Ibkha proved irresistibly powerful. He'd experienced this feeling of weakness before, accompanied by an overwhelming sense of loss for the things he'd hated, loved, renounced; in short, for all the components of his past.

It was with this assumption that Muhammad Ali Akbar hurried home, but by noon the next day none of the symptoms had shown signs of abating. When he attempted to rise from his mattress, he was amazed to find that he'd slept through until noon without awakening, and what shook him even more was that his sense of weakness persisted. In a state of fear, he tried to elucidate the cause, and saw himself standing by the seashore, almost blinded by the reflected glare of the sun on the water. The two waterskins were balanced on his shoulders, and he felt a debilitating weakness. The glare of the sun increased, but he found himself unable to close his burning eyes. He went back to sleep almost immediately.

From now on, time as people comprehend it became meaningless for Muhammad Ali Akbar. Everything that took place subsequently left him with the feeling that he was floating in the air, his legs dangling above the ground like a hanged man's. He was moving past the tableau of time, and as for the latter it could only be conceived as immobile, immovable as a mountain of basalt. His role as an active participant in life had ceased, and henceforth he was to become an onlooker. He felt disassociated and connected with nothing, he was removed from a world in which actions resembled fish browsing in a glass bowl, and he felt his deflated eyes were also composed of glass.

The next time he regained consciousness he found himself being carried away by men who supported his legs and arms. He was exhausted but summoned the strength to remember that he was without something important, and managed to articulate in a weak voice: "The box! The box!"

But no one took any notice of him. In despair, he made a futile effort to return to his box, and with visible urgency, gasped: "The box!"

Again no one paid him any attention.

They'd already arrived at the door, and he clung to the door and panted in a faint voice: "The box!"

Unable to bear the strain, he relapsed into a state of trance. This time he felt the tide slowly rising round his feet; the water was intensely cold and his hands were clinging to a square rock which was pulling him down. When he regained consciousness, he found himself hugging his old box, securely tied with its hemprope. He could see white shadows flitting to and fro, then a needle was stuck in his arm, and a face was leaning over him.

The days passed without meaning, although Muhammad Ali Akbar seemed to be frozen into the permanent severity of a pain that continued with or without his knowledge with unabating persistence. Everything merged into one: the sea with the low wooden latticed windows by the roadside, a pair of ceramic earrings with an *aba* soaked by the sea, and somewhere in the picture was a boat hanging motionless on the waves and an old wooden box.

Only once was he startled into a realization of the world, when he responded to a voice by his side enquiring: "What's in that old box?"

He looked towards the source of the voice, and saw, as if in a dream, a clean-shaven, fair-haired youth pointing at the box with insistent eyes.

But the moment of consciousness had been brief, and he'd gone back to staring mutely at the sea; yet the fair-haired youth with the clean-shaven face remained with him on the shore. After that he'd experienced a rare and sudden burst of energy. For no apparent reason everything had grown clear, and for the first time since his collapse he watched the sunrise clearly, and it seemed to him not impossible that he could leave his bed and return to doing errands on his bicycle. He felt reassured to find the box safely next to him, tied up as usual, but when he made a movement to get up, he was surprised to find himself the subject of scrutiny to a circle of white-coated men. He tried to say something, but was unable to, and felt that the tide had risen to his waist. The water had become so unbearably cold that it was numbing, and when he'd stretched out his arm to hold on to something for fear of drowning, everything had given way under his fingers. When he saw the face of the fair-haired youth again, he grew apprehensive about his box, and continued to stare at the youth's face until the water rose and obscured it from view.

"Bed 12 has died!" the nurse exclaimed.

I couldn't free myself of the image of Muhammad Ali Akbar's eyes staring at me before he died. I imagined that this man, who'd refused so resolutely to have his name truncated, might even settle for the conviction that he was Bed 12, if only he could rest assured of the fate of his box, if only he could...

This, my dear Ahmad, is the story of Muhammad Ali Akbar, or Bed 12, who died yesterday evening and is now laid out in the autopsy room, his body covered by a shroud. His is the lean, brown face which transferred the ulcer from my stomach to my head, and which made me write to you in the hope that you'll never again flippantly say to me: "I almost died laughing!"

Your brother

* * * * *

My dear Ahmad,

I'm still in the hospital. My health is progressing back to normal, and my way of finding this out is highly amusing.

Do you know how I test my strength?

I stand smoking on the balcony, and then see how far I can throw the butt into the green lanes of grass in the garden. In past weeks the butt would fall just short of the fourth lane, but now I can almost make it reach the sixth.

I understand from your letter that you don't feel the need to have witnessed Muhammad Ali Akbar's death in order to know what death is...you seem to feel that the event of death doesn't need all the tragic antecedents I assigned to it, and that people die with greater simplicity. The one who fell on the pavement while carrying a loaded gun, and had the bullet tear through his neck, was out at the time with an exquisitely beautiful girl. And the other one, who dropped dead from a heart attack on the road one April evening, had just got married the week before. All this is true, my dear Ahmad, I don't dispute it. However, that's not the point. The issue of death doesn't concern the dying. It's the concern of the living, who bitterly await their turn to be an example to expectant eyes. The main point of my last letter was to emphasize how necessary it is for us to transfer our thinking from the starting point of death...whether as in your opinion, the person dies while he's enjoying the charms of an exquisitely beautiful girl's body, or whether he dies staring at the clean-shaven face of a youth he's afraid of for the sake of his old wooden box tied up with rope. For the problem remains the problem of the end, whether it entails annihilation or immortality. Or what, my dear Ahmad?

Anyway, pouring water into a bag full of holes is a pointless exercise. Do you know what happened after I sent you my last letter? I went to the doctors' room and found them preparing a report on Muhammad Ali Akbar. They were about to open his box... My dear Ahmad, how much we're prisoners of our minds and bodies! We forever ascribe our own qualities to others, and judge them through the manner of our formulated thoughts and opinions. In short, we want them to be "us," we try to conceive of them as satellites of ourselves, we hope that they see with our eyes, feel with our skins, and in addition we attempt to saddle them with our past, and our own particular way of facing life, and place them within the framework which our current understanding of time and place dictates.

Muhammad Ali Akbar was none of the things I've mentioned. He was the father of three boys and two girls, for in his country men marry young. Nor had he been a water seller, since water's abundant in Oman. A long time ago, before settling here, he'd been a sailor on a sailboat that ran a line between the gulf ports and the South.

Muhammad Ali Akbar had been in Kuwait for four years, and after unsparingly fierce efforts had finally managed, only two months ago, to open what passed for a shop on one of the pavements of the New Road. How he supported his children in Oman remains a mystery.

I read in the doctor's report that the patient had gone blind six hours prior to his death, so I'm spared the disquieting thought that he was staring at me at the moment of death. The report also mentions that the family address of the patient is not known, so burial will proceed in the presence of the hospital undertakers only.

The doctor read the report in a loud voice to his colleagues, and the technical phraseology applied only to the nature of the illness, and not the patient. It was both precise and condensed, and delivered in an elegiac tone; then, when he'd finished reading it, he began untying the hemprope that bound the box. At this point I thought of leaving the room, for the matter didn't concern me. The Muhammad Ali Akbar that I knew had died. The one on whom they delivered a report was another person, and the box likewise belonged to that someone else. I knew only too well what was in Muhammad Ali Akbar's box, so what was the point of being inquisitive about some other matter?

However, curiosity overcame me, and I stood in a corner trembling with anticipation. The box was opened summarily, its contents examined by the doctor, and then it was discarded.

I looked apprehensively into the box. A collection of invoices relating to the shop's imported goods formed a solid wedge. In one corner there was an old picture of a bearded face, a frayed watch strap, a piece of rope, a small candle and a few rupees scattered among the papers. To tell you the truth I was disappointed, but before I left the room I saw something that stunned me. In pushing the invoices to one side, the nurse had upturned a pair of long ceramic earrings that flashed from the bottom of the box. My head spun, but I managed to walk over to the box and pick up the earrings for closer examination. I glanced at the nurse, and was suddenly compelled to say: "He bought these for Sabika! I'm sure he did!"

She stared at me, uncomprehendingly, then both she and the doctor laughed at what they took to be a joke.

You probably know that medics like to humor their ulcer patients for fear of a relapse.

Your brother